Taking Liberties

First Edition

Published by The Nazca Plains Corporation
Las Vegas, Nevada
2008

ISBN: 978-1-934625-65-1

Published by

The Nazca Plains Corporation ®
4640 Paradise Rd, Suite 141
Las Vegas NV 89109-8000

PUBLISHER'S NOTE
Taking Liberties is a work of fiction created wholly by *Christopher Trevor's* imagination. All characters are fictional and any resemblance to any persons living or deceased is purely by accident. No portion of this book reflects any real person or events.

Cover Photo, Jakub Wójtowicz
Art Director, Blake Stephens

Dedication

For Joe Lopes, a wonderful internet buddy and an outstanding friend, thanks for so much inspiration.

Taking Liberties

First Edition

Christopher Trevor

Contents

Introduction

Liberties, in modern time, are generally considered a concept of political philosophy and identify the condition in which an individual has the ability to act according to their own will.

That is the definition that Mr. Webster offers us in his famous book called the dictionary. But what if those liberties were taken to an extreme or even to an erotic level?

Individualist and liberal conceptions of liberties relate to the freedom of the individual from outside compulsion.

Again, that is Mr. Webster's definition of a person not having to deal with liberties being taken on them, or, to be more to the point, not to be taken harsh advantage of.

Positive liberty is often described as freedom to achieve certain ends, while negative liberty is described as from external coercion.

It is that external coercion that I am leading to herein, with this latest book, which has been aptly titled, “Taking Liberties.”

From my perspective I see “Taking Liberties” as sinister on the part of the taker and hapless and victimizing on the part of the one being taken liberties of…

OR, as my good buddy and constant tickle hero/victim, Timmy Backman would say:

“Taking Liberties”, well now, let’s see. Timmy Backman, my alter ego and preferred personality is in a constant state of having liberties taken with him. To take liberties, to me and the fictional Timmy means to go beyond the norm; over the top; to exceed normal boundaries, but then again, where Timmy is concerned what are normal boundaries? In all his experiences Timmy has had both men and women take liberties with his ticklishness, his gullibility, his sexiness, and his overstocked libido. These people and characters in Timmy’s various escapades have taken their liberties with his racy libido and they have erotically tortured and driven the poor boy to distraction and near sexual insanity. Timmy’s tormentors, or liberty takers, don’t seem to know that there are any boundaries with Timmy. They are under the impression that the norm is whatever they wish to do to the poor laddy, which mostly is to tickle and tease and sexually frustrate him…the poor guy. And Timmy gets taken over the top; he has liberties taken with him over and over again. In fact, Timmy might as well have a sign tattooed on his forehead that reads “Do me. Whatever you want to do…just do me!” And believe me his tormentors and liberty takers show no respect for boundaries as they “take their liberties” and feel free to satisfy their sexual whims at Timmy’s expense…

Now, in Christopher Trevor’s latest book read how a well muscled jock has liberties taken with him by an oversexed orderly while in an examination room. A painter, hired by an editor has a very delectable part of him become the main course for an afternoon delight and I myself become the main ingredient in a huge salad at a fundraising event, all in the name of "Taking Liberties." And those are just a few tidbits of what Mr. Trevor this time out...has in store for us...

So as the author usually says, "Happy Reading..."

Taking Liberties

When I was in college and studying for my medical degree I worked part-time in a medical facility as an orderly, a doctor's and nurse's assistant and just all around go-for, (a gopher if you would.) It was the kind of facility that housed offices for various doctors. There was a pediatrician, a general practitioner, a neurologist and an orthopedic. It was the orthopedic, Dr. Carlson that I was working for those few days when the incident that I want to tell you about happened. Looking back on it now I still can't believe it happened, and I often wonder where the golden haired Brad Silvers is now…

It was the mid nineteen seventies, thirty years ago or more, at best. I was on room clean-up duty, the job entailing that after the doctor had finished with his current patient in the examining room I was to go in the room and freshen it up. I would have to have fresh tissue paper stretched across the examining table, make sure all instrument wrappers were placed in the wastebaskets and to be VERY sure that all used syringes, tongue depressors and other body search materials were disposed of in separate garbage receptacles. A tidy office, that's what the doctors at the facility that I worked for insisted upon. Dressed in my all white uniform of an orderly's style button up at the sides pull-over shirt, loose fitting white string-tied pants, white sneakers and white sweat socks I made my way down the hall toward room 2008, where one Brad Silvers had just been to see the orthopedic, Dr. Carlson. The supervising nurse had told me to clean up the room because the doctor had another patient that would need the facility within an hour or so. As I walked toward the room I snapped on a pair of latex gloves, seeing as the first items to be chucked in the garbage were always the body cavity search items. Thinking that the room was vacant I entered without knocking and as I opened the door I heard a husky voice call out, "Oh shit!!" Startled, I let the door of the room slam closed behind me and I instantly looked toward where the voice had come from, straight ahead and in front of me. He was on the examination table, the most beautiful fucking sight I had seen in all my twenty-something years. Stretched out on his back, wearing nothing but a pair of white Fruit of the Loom briefs (remember this was the 1970's) and calf length white sweat socks I saw that he was tethered to the examination table with leather straps fastened at his wrists with his muscular arms at his sides and at his spread out calves, the straps fastened just above his socked ankles. I nearly gasped at the sight of him and my cock started to instantly rise to the occasion in my loose fitting orderly's pants…

"Oh, uh, sorry, I didn't know anyone was in here," I said, trying to sound as stupid as possible.

"Well now you know man," he barked at me, his head turned as he faced me and I approached the examination table he was mounted on.

From the way his muscular and well shaped legs were bent back and his knees were pointing at the ceiling I guessed his height to be around nearly six feet or better. His socked feet looked to be around size eleven or so. My mouth filled with saliva at the sight of those huge jock boy feet and I quickly gulped it down. His upper body was a muscular work of God's art. He was shaped like an Adonis, and Michael Angelo could not have sculpted anything better. He had hard looking washboard abs, totally ripped, his chest and pecs were hugely muscular. They were the kind of pecs that bounced involuntarily when he would talk. And on that rock hard chest two of the most delectable and fleshy looking nipples I had ever seen. All day suckers I call nipples like that, whether they are on a man or a woman's chest. Fuck, when it comes to a pair of suck-able looking tits I don't discriminate man, male or female, tits is tits is my motto. His shoulders were broad and they were as wide as a doorway and his arms were hugely muscular with curved and well-developed biceps and triceps. As I then stood at the side of the table he was well strapped to I saw that he was nervously clenching and unclenching his hands into and out of fists. His hands were the size of hams and those fists looked big and strong enough to punch holes through walls with. His eyes were piercingly blue and he had golden blond wavy hair. His muscular and well toned body was smooth as a baby's bottom, not a speck of hair on him, lick-able as I would call it, a feast fit for a king, or a degenerate like me, HA, HA. I guessed his age to be somewhere in the vicinity of mine, early twenties or thereabouts.

"The uh, the supervising nurse told me to come in here and clean up the room," I said to the blond muscle god. "She said room 2008 needed cleaning for the next patient coming in, in an hour or so…"

"Well obviously the stupid bitch didn't know that I was still in here," the blond jock boy looking guy said harshly, obviously embarrassed at having been found in such a sexy and vulnerable position. "Doctor Carlson had to step out for a bit, said he would be back for me when the injection he gave me took effect. He said it would take about twenty minutes or so to a half hour, that way he could see other patients in the meanwhile, jeez…"

"What uh, what kind of injection did he give you?" I asked, looking hungrily at those nipples of his that were now half erect on his smooth and muscular chest.

"Some sort of antibiotic mixed with a pain killer, I'm the captain of the football team at Stanford College," the strapped down jock went on.

Just as I thought, a jock boy, what I sometimes refer to as "dumb" jock boys…

"We had a game today and I was tackled pretty hard and I twisted my left calf," he went on. "The pain was pretty bad but I was still able to walk…"

I looked at him again as stupidly as possible and said, "So????"

"So my coach insisted that I have the calf checked out by an orthopedic doctor, hence the reason I'm here," he went on and blew out an exasperated sounding breath. "Total waste of fucking time if you ask me man…"

I quickly looked around the room and saw that his football uniform knickers, jersey, cleats, protective equipment, meaning his crotch cup (YUM) and helmet were piled up on a chair.

"Oh, so they brought you here directly from the field huh?" I asked him after surveying his pile-up of clothes.

"Oh man, a smart one," he grunted.

I saw some light looking bruises on his legs and one on his right arm, obviously badges of honor from when he had been tackled…

Ignoring his snide remark about me I asked him why he was tethered to the examining table. With a look on his face that told me he thought I was the dumbest orderly in creation he told me that because of the pain in his calf the doctor didn't want him moving around and running the risk of injuring himself even more-so.

"Is that easy enough for you to understand?" he asked me.

"Yeah, sure, I suppose so," I replied and as I glanced at the briefs he was wearing I saw a small wet spot form there.

My mouth again filled with saliva…and I gulped it down…

"Your uh, your name is Brad Silvers, right?" I asked him.

"Yep, just like it says there on the chart," he replied, gesturing with his head and chin at the table across from the one he was on where all medical instruments were.

"I'm Ron," I said to him.

"Nice to meet you Ron," Brad said sarcastically. "I would shake your hand but as you can see I'm a little tied up at the moment."

At that remark we both grinned and laughed good naturedly…

"Fuckin' doctor, when he told me he had to strap me up like this I didn't do a damned thing to stop him," the jock said, sounding irritated as all hell. "I guess I have some sort of masochistic tendencies huh Ron?"

"No, I think you were just doing well to do what the doctor said," I replied.

"Yeah, yeah, whatever," Brad replied.

"So do you think your calf is really injured?" I asked him, an evil plan formulating in my head.

"Nah, but I got to do as my coach says man," Brad Silvers said. "If I don't I could be thrown off the team and even lose my football scholarship."

"I see," I said. "So the doctor said he would be back in a half hour huh?"

“Something like that,” the football jock said. “And man, its one thing for him to have left me strapped up in just my under shorts and socks, but he should have locked that door you know?”

“I’ll take care of that right now,” I said.

“Thanks man,” Brad said and he was obviously thinking that I would lock the door on my way out.

When he saw me latch the door from the inside and then step back to the table he was strapped to was when the look of confusion came over his angelically yet ruggedly handsome face…

“Why uh, why didn’t you lock it from outside after you left?” he asked, seeing the hunger in my eyes. “I’m sure the doctor has a key man…”

“Is the injection that the doctor gave you having any kind of side effects?” I asked him. “Something I could possibly help you out with?”

“What do you mean?” he asked, sounding a bit nervous now.

“Well, some medications can have strange side effects, some of them can even act as an aphrodisiac,” I responded, gesturing toward his crotch and the semi erection that was outlined erotically in his white briefs.

The wet spot had grown a tad larger at that point and the slit of his cock was visible through his briefs.

“You don’t have to be embarrassed about it, a lot of medications have that kind of effect,” I went on.

“Oh, uh, no, no, I just uh, nothing like that man, I just have to piss,” Brad Silvers said and I saw my golden (pun intended) opportunity. “As soon as the doc gets back and takes the straps off me I’ll use the bathroom and…"

"I can actually help you with that right now," I said eagerly, reached under the table he was on and held up a bedpan.

"You have got to be kidding bud!!" Brad Silvers said in shock as I stepped next to his crotch.

"No problem at all Brad, no reason why you should have to lay there feeling uncomfortable because you have to urinate," I said, sounding as dumb as possible.

Then, before he could say another word I was working at getting his huge manhood through the fly opening of his briefs. As I did so I also, just for the fuck of it brought out his huge juicy testicles, DAMN, they were the size of golf balls and all randy smelling. His briefs were sort of wet with sweat and his cock was a tad more than semi hard by then, his tube steak was of the jumbo size, and he was very gifted in that area I must say. As I took it gently in hand he gasped breathlessly as I held it over the bedpan. It was hot and pulsing, all eight to nine inches of it. The green veins on his rod-like shaft were paramount and throbbing with a life of their own as well.

"OOOOOOO got me by the cock man, I-I can't piss like that bud," Brad swooned as I gave the tip of his cock a few twitches to try to get him spewing his golden juice. "I, I get real pee shy if someone is watching me, and as you can see I'm tellin' the truth here. I won't be able to piss in that bedpan you got there; no matter how bad I really need to…"

"I can help you with that as well Brad," I said with a mean looking grin on my face.

I dropped the bedpan to the floor, and still holding his throbber in hand I leaned down and slurped the very tip of it between my lips.

"H-holy fuck and fucking fuck," Brad Silvers seethed as I

caressed his piss slit with the tip of my tongue. “What in all hell are you doing man??? OH FUCK…”

I nodded my head up and down, squeezed his shaft and slathered my tongue again over his slit, and lo and behold, a second later he was pissing…and pissing…and pissing….

“OHHHHHHHH, oh man, fucking perv you are, you’re scoffing down my damned piss Ron,” the jock panted. “You do this for all the patients here???”

He snickered meanly and when he tried to thrust more of his cock into my mouth I held it tight, preventing him from doing so…I knew I had scored here… His golden juice tasted sour, vile and a bit like rotten lemons. But he was made by the gods and because of that I eagerly and anxiously drank down his offering…

When he was done pissing I took his cock tip from my mouth and licked my lips. I stood up straight and he looked at me in total disbelief.

“Fuck man, holy fucking shit, you just drank down my rancid piss,” Brad Silvers intoned, sounding somewhat angry yet relieved at the same time.

“No problem Brad,” I said with a grin.

“No problem??? No fucking problem??? Just what in the fuck was that all about man???” the jock bantered, squirming in the straps that held him fast.

I noticed as I moved over to his upper torso that he hadn’t asked me to pack him back into his briefs. I had purposely left his manhood and huge testicles on display for the fun to come…or cum if you prefer…

“So I suppose you’re not all that pee shy after all huh?” I asked him, reached down and tweaked one of his big erect nipples, giving it a twist as I mashed it a bit between my thumb and first two fingers.

"Fuck, what in the hell do you think you're doin' here man? Takin' liberties with me?" Brad grunted throatily. "Fucker, take your damned hand off my tit and…UHHHHHH!!!"

But before he could finish his sentence I had leaned down and slurped his other nebulous nipple into my mouth. As I slurped the nipple of his that I had between my front-most teeth I twirled and whirled the tip of his other one with my fingers and thumb.

"AWWWWW you fucking pervert man," Brad grunted, lifted his head a bit and watched as I made sport of licking, slurping and sucking on his nipple that was closest to me.

While I suctioned his tit with my mouth I used my fingers and thumb to erotically torment and stimulate his other nub.

"OH jeez man, I see you losing your goddamned job over this Ron ol' boy," the football jock threatened, yet he hadn't yelled out for help as I worked him over.

After a while I stopped working his nipple with my fingers and thumb but continued slurping and sucking the other one. The one in my mouth had stiffened and the tip of it was as hard as a new pencil eraser.

"HUHHHHH, th-that feels real weird now, the way you're workin' just one of my big tits, SHIT…" Brad panted and heaved his chest upward.

With my hand now freed from toying with his other nipple I reached down and cupped his sweaty and juicy balls in my hand.

"UHHHHHHHH, f-fuck, those are my family jewels you got in your hand there Ron," he swooned as I fondled his balls between my fingers.

A few moments later I was leaning down on the other side of the examination table, Brad Silvers' other nipple now wedged in between my front-most teeth.

"UUUUUUUHHHHH, didn't want my other tit to feel left out huh pervert?" he asked me meanly as I again cupped his balls in my hand.

I fondled his balls, kissed and licked and slurped and sucked his other nipple and the jock boy rewarded me by grunting and panting in ecstasy…

"OOOOOO, fuck man, if the guys on my football team saw you doin' this to me they would make short work of you Ron," Brad threatened.

I momentarily stopped sucking his nipple, held his balls tight and looked at him as I said, "Or maybe those guys on your football team would either want to join me in what I'm doing here, or maybe, just maybe, they would want me to do to them what I'm doing to you muscle boy…"

"FUCK YOU!! FUCK YOU MAN!!!" Brad Silvers seethed in my face. "If you're goin' to suck my damned tits then suck my damned tits! Nothin' I can do about it anyways, but leave my buds out of this, GOT IT???"

"Yes Sir," I snickered, leaned down and slurped his nipple back into my mouth.

"OHHHHHHH, fucker, if I wasn't all strapped up like this we would see just how anxious you were to be usin' me like you are for your perverted pleasures…"

His verbal rant only spurred me on all the more to tease and taste the muscled jock boy…

When his nipples were both sucked up to hard and erect positions I slowly trailed my tongue down his midsection, kissing his chest, pecs and stomach areas as I went. When I stuck my tongue into his belly button and sucked at it he thrashed on the examination table and laughed a bit as he claimed that I was tickling his damned belly button…

I then stood up straight and stepped to the end of the examination table.

“What now man?” he asked, watching helplessly as I looked hungrily at his huge white socked feet. “My feet huh? You a foot freak too, besides being a damned tit freak? Fucker man, you signed your death warrant when you kissed, kissed and kissed me just now! Sucking a guy’s tits is one thing but kissin’ him is a horse of a whole other color!”

Snickering meanly I leaned down and sniffed his left socked foot, really sniffing in the scent emanating from his toes.

“Yeah, I knew it man, takin’ liberties with my damned feet now too, JEEZ!” he grunted and laid his head back as I knelt at the foot of the examination table.

I pressed my nose and mouth against the bottom of his dangling left foot and inhaled deeply, licked the socked bottom of it and kissed it over and over…

“Hey man, what in the fucking fuck did I just say to you about kissin’ me here?” he blubbered and I could hear the straps grinding against the bed as he struggled to get his hands freed…to no avail of course.

He could rant and swear all he wanted about how much he hated what I was doing to him, taking liberties as he called it, but there was no denying the state that his cock was in. He was harder than steel and from the way he was dripping droplets of pre seed I knew that he could cum at any second. But I was not yet going to give him that pleasure. If

I knew Dr. Carlson right, he would not be back in a half hour to tend to his patient, more like it would be an hour, which gave me all the time I needed to really feast on this hunk of beef…

I sniffed both his socked feet alternately; they smelled all musty, football player sweaty and grimy. By now my cock had stiffened to epic proportions in my orderly pants and soon I would need some relief. Glancing up at his dangling balls and erect cock I mulled over what else lay within the treasure chest called his briefs…

As I was peeling his socks from his feet he lifted his head and bantered some more at me, asking, "Hey man, hey Ron, what the fucking fuck??? Why are you taking my damned socks off me huh?"

As soon as his feet were bared he snickered with a snide looking grin on his face and said, "Yeah, I knew it, I just fucking knew it," as I slurped two of his little toes into my mouth and held his left foot in my hands like it was the holy grail.

"Fucker man, you're a freak for me," Brad Silvers taunted me meanly as I then slathered my tongue across the bottom of his foot that I had in my hand, sucking his big toe every few seconds.

"Jeez, hate to admit it but I can feel that in my cock when you suck my damned toe," the jock prattled. "Pervert, you're lucky my feet are all strapped up like they are, otherwise I would kick you in the face…"

"Does your calf hurt at all?" I asked him in between servicing his feet and sucking his toes.

"Nah, it feels good actually man," he said.

I smiled and moved over to his other foot. As I held him by the ankle I slurped his pinky toe into my mouth and sucked it vigorously.

"OHHHHHHHHH, fuck, but that's amazing you pervert," the

muscled jock swooned, rocking his head back and forth on the table. "Never thought my toes were so damned sexy sensitive…got to get my girl to do these things for me…"

I nearly burst out laughing at that comment…but instead I tossed his socks over to the chair where his other clothing was piled and stood in front of him, really taking in the sight of him from the feet up…

When he saw me lowering my orderly style pants to around my thighs a look of trepidation came over his beguilingly handsome face…

"H-hey man, what're you up to now?" the jock boy asked me as he saw my throbbing hard cock and low hanging balls. "AW no, no, you've got to be joking now…"

As I brought out the section of the table to place his feet in the stirrups he looked helplessly toward the door to the room.

"No man, the doc, he'll be coming in here any second and if he catches you with your goddamned cock up my ass you'll be fired for sure," the footballer pleaded.

"Ah, so you know what I have in mind for you next eh my jock boy?" I teased him meanly.

He looked across at me as I untied his feet, slid his underpants off him and quickly slipped his feet into the stirrups and locked them in at the ankles. There wasn't much he could do to stop me, seeing as his wrists were tightly fastened to the sides of the examination table he was on.

"Oh fuck, oh no man," he gurgled as I turned the lever that would raise his feet and put his glorious hole on display for me.

"If you scream out for help I'll gag you with your socks," I threatened him.

"FUCK YOU again man, I'm no pansy, I won't scream like a girl for help," he railed.

When his bunghole was staring me upwards in the face I let my mouth fill with a hearty amount of saliva…

"Hope you're ready for this jock boy," I said teasingly.

"And I hope you're ready for this, when I'm not tied up anymore I'm gonna make short work of you Ron, you fucking perv man," he grated at me.

I hocked up a goodly amount of saliva and spit twice into his hole…

"PWAHHH!!" was the sound I made as I started using my spit to lube his shit chute.

"Fucking bastard," Brad Silvers grunted a few moments later when I was spitting directly into his anal canal, kneeling in front of him and practically dribbling my saliva in there.

His hole seemed to be sucking up my mouth juices. He could swear and curse all he wanted but somewhere inside him he loved what I was doing to him… I then pressed my lips against the walls of his hole and he swooned and swore like a captured marine, sweating now atop the table he was on.

"Fucker, I should rip a good smelly fart right in your face," Brad Silvers said meanly.

"You do that and I will gag you with your socks," I responded and spit a few more times into his hole, really sopping it well with my saliva.

A few minutes later I licked and flicked my tongue around inside his anal walls, treating his chamber like it was a pussy and then, primed and prepped, he was ready for my entrance… He gurgled from deep down in his chest and his massive pecs bounced involuntarily as I then fingered his soaked hole, prodding it first with one digit, then a second and I swear he squeaked in a high-pitched tone when I slid a third finger inside him. He was all squishy back there and ready for an even bigger invasion…

"Bastard, pervert," Brad Silvers whispered helplessly then as I slowly slid my fingers from his most private crevice.

His hole was literally twitching as I stood up at the entrance of it…

"Please man, suckin' my tits and worshipping my feet was one thing, kissing me was another," Brad Silvers pleaded. "But fucking me is off limits and…UHHHHHHH!!!!"

Before he could again finish what he was saying I took my liberties with him, as I slid my steely hard rod inside him…

The walls of his hole seemed to suck my cock in as far as possible…

"AWWWWWWWW you bastard, you skunk man," the footballer grunted, clenched his huge hands into fists and squeezed his eyes shut as I began slowly thrusting in and out of him, holding to his raised ankles as I did so. "OHHHHHHHH NO, no, not this…oh my poor asshole!!!"

I got a good rhythm going as I held tight to his ankles, kissed his bare feet and slid in and out and in and out of his sopping wet lubricated bunghole.

"You'll pay for this Ron, and so will that doctor for leaving me here all tied up, making me into easy pickins for the likes of you," Brad seethed, yet somehow he was thrusting with me back there.

"Pay for it man?" I asked him teasingly. "Fucking muscle boy,

I'm getting all this for free, and then some…HOOOOOOO yeah…"

I slammed into him real hard so that my pubic bush was matted against his anal entrance.

"OHHHHHHHH…GAWD, I-I think I'm gonna pop my load you pervert, you sleazy bastard," Brad Silvers cried and then, to my utter and total disbelief he spewed forth a few jettisons of cum from his throbbing cock, without even having his member touched.

"Fuck, can't believe I'm seeing that with my own eyes," I panted breathlessly as I slid in him again, his asshole walls hugging my cock, me feeling like I was about to cum any second as well. "You love this man, you just came like a fucking whore on a Saturday night and I didn't even touch your goddamned crank…"

"Yeah? Well I feel like you're touching my goddamned shit now man," he panted up at me, screeching almost at that point. "I'm all sensitive and sexy feeling after I shoot my load fucker! Translation, get your fucking rod out of me now!! GAWWWWDDD!!!"

As he ranted and raved I shot my load deep inside him, he cried like a girl as my warm juices flooded him deep and intensely…

When I slid out of him my cock was flaccid and I looked at him adoringly, the blond used up muscle god of a footballer…

He lay there panting and catching his breath as I finished him off by licking and eating all his cum off his stomach area, where it had all landed when he'd shot his pent-up load…

"I'll get you for this Ron," he said to me as I wiped his tears off his face, using his sweaty underpants of all things.

"Yeah, I bet you will man, fuck, I'll even leave my home address in the pocket of your football knickers over there," I teased him. "Then when you get to my place we'll see how you're begging for more of what I just did to you…I would be willing to bet you'll even beg me to tie you the fuck up when the time comes…"

"You're sick man, we'll see about that," he ranted back at me.

A short while later I had the muscled jock back in the position he had been in when I first came into his room. I had even put his socks back on his feet. He lay there in his underpants, still strapped tight to the examination table.

"Anyway, I'll go and see what's keeping Dr. Carlson," I snickered and hefted my pants back up as I left the examination room, my cock still tingling after the trip it had taken down the sweet jock boy's chute.

I glanced over at his football knickers and knew he would show up at my place at some point…

When I got to the reception area I asked the young lady on duty if she knew what was keeping Dr. Carlson, explaining how he had a patient waiting for him in room 2008. She told me that Dr. Carlson would be delayed another half hour or so, explaining that he'd had an unexpected emergency to attend to. She asked me if the patient in room 2008 was comfortable. I smiled and told her that I would go in there and make sure that he was…

When I entered room 2008 again Brad Silvers shivered at the sight of me, he cringed as I again locked the door from the inside and went to work on him a second time, starting again with his suck-able jutted up nipples…

He swore again like a captured marine…

Having My Home Office Painted

My name is Steve Harley; I work as an editor for various magazines and one publishing company. Being that as it is I am able to work from home. Thank God for computers and the internet huh? Well, my home office was in dire need of a good paint job. I had been promising myself that I would get the place painted. It had been more than two years since I had it painted and the guy who had painted it back then was no longer available. When I called his cell phone number I got a recording saying that the number had been disconnected and that there was no further information or even a new number that he could be reached at. Ah well, people do move on and I simply figured I would either have to find someone new to paint for me or do it myself. The place really needed it let me tell you. But with my job keeping me so busy it was just about impossible to take the time to try to find a guy to hire. Being that I am not that good at painting was the main reason I preferred to have it done by someone who knew what they were doing. While I was at the offices of the publishing company that I work for picking up some new assignments I had asked a few buddies of mine if they knew anyone who painted professionally or just very well, explaining that I needed a small room in my apartment done and that I basically sucked at painting. Two of them said that the porter named Eddie had painted their offices there at the company and that they were very satisfied with his work.

"How much does he charge?" I asked Rocco, a big muscular guy of thirty something years old.

"He's reasonable, nice guy too," Rocco said as I signed some papers for him, release forms for work that I would be taking home with me. "He started working here a month or so ago and he made it clear that he does part-time work for people, stuff like painting for instance. He also does minor home repairs if you need anything like that done, outdoor stuff too. He doesn't mind being able to make a little extra cash on the side from time to time."

"Perfect, he sounds like just the kind of guy I'm looking for," I said.

I asked Rocco where I could find Eddie and as he looked at the clock on his office wall he said that more than likely Eddie would be in the company cafeteria at this time, having lunch.

"What does he look like?" I asked.

"Afro-American guy, he's in his mid to late thirties, short cropped hair, nicely built, dark eyes, reasonably good looking," Rocco said.

"Cool man, I appreciate this," I said

I thanked Rocco, shook his hand, thanked him also for the work and headed to the cafeteria. As I got off the elevator in the concourse level of the office building where the company cafeteria was the scent of cooking wafted through the air. I figured while I was there I may as well have some lunch as well. But first I had to find Eddie and see about hiring him to paint my home office. I hoped he would be available during one of the next two weekends. My home office can be painted inside of one day, a few hours at most. I would need the night before of course to move everything out of there first. And then moving it all back in after the paintjob was done was the real tedious work…

I walked into the cafeteria and looked around for a black guy dressed as a porter…

He was seated by himself at a back table. He was clad in the navy blue porter's uniform of pants and matching short sleeved button down shirt with the company logo etched on the breast pocket.

"Eddie?" I asked when I was standing by the table he was seated at.

"Yes?" he asked, looking up from the newspaper he had been reading.

"I'm sorry, I don't mean to interrupt you, I'm Steve Harley, I'm an editor here at the company, I work from home," I said, my hand held out.

"Oh yes, I've heard of you," Eddie said, his hand outstretched and shook mine in a tight grip. "What can I do for you?"

"Well, I need a small room in my apartment painted and Rocco in the editorial department said that you sometimes do part time work like that," I said as Eddie continued pumping my hand, finally letting go a few seconds later. "Would you be interested in a painting job for say, three hundred dollars?"

"Yeah, I do painting and other household things for people," Eddie said.

"So you would be interested?" I asked again. "This coming weekend if that's not too short notice? The room I need painted can be done in less than one day, it is that small."

"It would have to be Sunday," Eddie said. "I have a job already on Saturday that I have to do," Eddie said. "I painted this ladies' living room recently, and now she wants her bedroom done… The lady *likes me*, if you know what I mean…"

He winked at me, a mischievous look in his dark eyes.

"Yeah, I think I know what you mean," I said, grinning at him.

"So, Sunday it is?" Eddie asked.

"Okay, Sunday sounds fine, that'll give me time to clear all the furniture and the computer out of there," I said as I sat down across from him for a moment. "I'll give you my address and phone number…"

I wrote my address and phone number on a piece of yellow legal paper from a pad that I keep in my attaché case and handed it to Eddie.

"Okay Mr. Harley, what time should I be there?" Eddie asked after looking at the paper with my information on it.

"Around noon should be good," I said. "Does that work for you?"

"Sure does," Eddie replied. "You have paintbrushes, rollers, mats to put down on the floor, a ladder all that stuff?"

"Yes, I do, and I'll buy the paint during the week, I'm figuring two large cans should suffice for the entire room," I said.

"Good, I have extras on all that stuff which I'll bring with me, along with my painting clothing," Eddie said.

Once we were done talking Eddie said his lunch hour was over and that he had to get back to work. I shook hands with him again, said

I would see him that coming Sunday and went to get some lunch for myself…

Sunday rolled around and by eleven thirty I had all the furniture and the computer out of my home office. My living room looked like a bomb had hit it however, seeing as that was where I had piled all the stuff from my home office room. I made sure that the air conditioner in my home office was turned up good and high, seeing as it was ninety-eight degrees that day, with nearly one hundred percent humidity to boot. Actually I had all the air conditioners in my apartment turned up real high. For the summer months one doesn't care how much the electric bill is going to come to, comfort is what counts. Around ten to twelve my doorbell rang and I let Eddie into the apartment…

"Hey there Mr. Harley," Eddie said as we shook hands. "Good morning…"

"Good morning Eddie," I said and closed the door after he let go of my hand. "And please, call me Steve, there's no need to be so formal…"

"Sounds good to me Steve," Eddie said and put down the large gym bag he was carrying, which contained painting utensils and such.

Eddie was clad in blue jeans, white sneakers and a pull-over white tee shirt…

"Where can I change into my painting gear?" Eddie asked, bending down to pull a pair of white paint-scuffed workpants out of his gym bag along with a paint smeared tee shirt.

"Uh, bathroom is right over there," I said, pointing. "Or you can just change in the room you'll be painting…"

"I'll change in the bathroom," Eddie said and stepped into the bathroom, closing the door behind him.

"Can I get you a cold drink or something?" I called out to him.

"Iced tea or some club soda would hit the spot," Eddie called back from behind the closed bathroom door. "It's hot as hell out there today…"

A few moments later he emerged from the bathroom wearing his white khaki paint-scuffed work pants rolled up at the ankles over his sneakers and white sweat socks and a black paint smeared tee shirt which I noticed was pretty form fitting. The guy had a muscular body, nicely defined, not overdone though. I handed him the glass of iced tea and as he sipped it down he looked around my living room where all the stuff from my home office was strewn and stacked up.

"Nice place you have here Steve," Eddie said.

"Yes, I like it, but at some point I have to find something bigger, the work is really starting to pile up, but I until I can afford it this will have to do," I said. "Like most people I've accumulated a lot of stuff through the years."

"I can see that," Eddie said and we both laughed good naturedly.

"I suppose you can call me a packrat or I can say I need all this stuff for research," I added as Eddie looked around.

"Nice high ceilings too," Eddie commented, looking upwards. "I hope you have a ladder in your home office that reaches that high for when I have to paint the ceiling."

"Oh yes, definitely, come, I'll show you," I said, taking Eddie by his upper arm and walking with him toward the room that was my home office.

"These houses were built pre-war, as they call them," I said. "Back then they built them with very high ceilings…"

In the home office I had placed drop cloths all over the floor, completely covering it. The floor in my home office is sandblasted to a high sheen and I did not want any paint droppings getting on it. Eddie sipped his iced tea and looked around the room as I held his arm in a friendly manner. On the floor were two cans of light blue colored paint that would be used for the walls along with one can of white paint for the ceiling. Next to the cans of paint were a can of turpentine and some rags along with one long basin for the blue paint and one long basin for the white paint that Eddie could pour the paint into. Next to that I had set out various sized paintbrushes, rollers and such.

"Hmm, cool, it looks like I didn't have to bring all that stuff that I have out there in my gym bag," Eddie said and gulped down the rest of his iced tea. "Do you have some masking tape that I can use to put along the border between the ceiling and the walls? I don't want any white paint getting on your blue walls or vice versa."

I let go of Eddie's arm and snapped my fingers in frustration, saying that I knew that there had been something I'd forgotten. Eddie grinned a lady-killer smile that showed off pearly white teeth and said not to worry, that he had masking tape in his gym bag. Against a wall was a high extension ladder that would make it easy for Eddie to reach the ceiling when he painted it. The humming sound of the air conditioner filled the room…

"Okay then, it looks like I'm all set to go here," Eddie said, handing me his empty glass. "I'll just get some masking tape from my bag and get started…"

"Sounds like a plan to me Eddie," I said and together we walked out of my home office.

I walked to the kitchen to put the glass in the dishwasher as Eddie opened his gym bag to get some masking tape…

When I came back to my home office Eddie was on the top step of the ladder sticking masking tape along the border just between the ceiling and the wall. When he couldn't reach anymore he slowly descended from the ladder, moved it a few feet to the next section he would have to tape and climbed to the top step.

"Do you want me to help you out Eddie?" I asked him as he did his work.

"No, I have this well in hand Mr. Harl-er-Steve, I can manage from here," Eddie replied.

"Okay, I'll be out in the living room looking over some printed projects that I need to work on," I said. "If you need anything just give a shout…"

"Will do Steve," Eddie said, smiling down at me from his perch on the ladder.

I stepped out of my home office and sat down on the couch in my living room to look over some of the paperwork that I had picked up at the office the previous week…

While I was sitting there I heard the ladder again being moved and this time Eddie called out to me. I sauntered into the home office and saw that he now had the ladder situated against a corner of the room.

"Would you mind holding the ladder for me this time Steve?" Eddie asked me. "When I do the corner borders the ladder is at an angle and I'm a little nervous it may not be well balanced."

"Sure thing," I said and as he climbed up the ladder I propped one of my feet on the second step of it and held it tight at the sides.

"Thanks Steve," Eddie said as he climbed with the masking tape in his hand.

"No problem," I said and glanced up as he continued climbing.

It was at that moment that things started to move in what seemed like slow motion. Looking upwards I could not help but notice that Eddie's backside looked like two well-shaped cantaloupes in his khaki workpants. As he ascended the ladder his two cheeks wiggled very sexily, almost like a woman's, I swear. My heart started racing at that sight and I could see a small sweat stain at the very center of the back of his pants. Suddenly I could not believe the thoughts that were going through my head. I climbed up a step or two and held tight to the sides of the ladder as Eddie stretched his muscular arms out to stick masking tape along the border. I could see his bushy armpits under the sleeves of his tee-shirt as he worked.

"Are you uh, doing okay up there Eddie?" I asked him, watching as his ass cheeks twitched a bit each time he moved about on the ladder step.

Straight as I am I have to admit it was somehow a glorious sight that well shaped ass of the painter's.

"Yeah, I'm okay, just that the air conditioner doesn't seem to cool it off way up here, I'm sweating a bit," Eddie said, but not in a complaining manner.

"Hmm, when we're off this ladder I'll take a look at it and see if I can increase the airflow for you," I said and this time Eddie glanced down as I spoke and I think he caught me staring at the wet spot on the back of his work pants.

He grinned down at me and said he was almost done, turned his back and resumed his work with the masking tape…

When he was done and as he was descending the ladder again I walked over to the air conditioner. I turned the dial to the highest setting and then the worst happened. The air conditioner made a sputtering sort of sound and then it went completely dead.

"What the hell?" I said, pressing the on/off button repeatedly, getting no response whatsoever from the device.

"Maybe you're pulling too much power," Eddie said. "Do you have a lot of electric appliances being used right now?"

"Yeah, but the electricity should be able to handle it," I said, continuing to press the on/off button on the damned air conditioner.

"Well, maybe this is an old unit you have here," Eddie said, moving the ladder to the next location. "Do you have a fan or something you can put in here? I can't work in this heat, unless I was in shorts of course, and I didn't bring any of those…"

With a look of helplessness on my mug I looked at Eddie and nodded "No", telling him that I did not have a fan. Shit, when one has air conditioning in every room of the house one doesn't need old fashioned fans.

"Well, I can lend you a pair of my shorts if that's okay with you," I said.

Eddie held up a hand and said that he did not want to do that, citing as he would probably get paint on them. I started having visions of my home office not being painted that day. The vision of Eddie's well shaped ass also kept playing in my mind. As he stood there getting sweatier now I could see how his black tee shirt was sticking to his torso. His nipple tips were paramount against the front of his shirt, nipple tips bigger than a woman's it seemed.

"It's okay if you get paint on the shorts Eddie," I began. "I really need this room painted and…"

Again Eddie held up a hand. "I'll deal," he said. "The same thing happened at the woman's house where I worked, the one I told you really liked me, and I dealt."

"How?" I asked him.

"Just pull down all the shades in here and I'll deal," Eddie replied. "She was aghast at first, but hell, I got her room painted and a nice bonus at the same time..."

As he stood there watching I pulled down the shades over the three windows in my home office.

"Okay, I'll get back to work now, when I reach the next corner to be masking taped I'll call you again to hold the ladder," Eddie said and as I turned to walk out of the home office I could swear that out of the corner of my eye I saw that he was unbuttoning his pants button.

I resumed working on my projects in the living room, looking over folders of stuff and such. About fifteen minutes later I heard Eddie calling my name. I called out that I was coming and when I walked into the home office he was just getting the ladder situated in an unbalanced sort of fashion against the next corner of the room. I stopped dead in my tracks as I watched Eddie begin to ascend the ladder. The fucking guy was wearing nothing but his scrungy white sweat socks tucked down around his ankles. I gaped for a moment at the sight of his black sexy ass, as I said, shaped like two hard cantaloupes. Also, through the back of his slightly parted thighs I saw his meaty balls hanging down real temptingly in his sac.

"Sorry about this Steve, but it is hot as hell in here, and we are both guys after all and..."

Eddie began.

"It, uh, it, it's fine," I said, staring at his ass cheeks as he climbed the ladder halfway. "It, its fine...just fine..."

Fine was the word bud, that ass of his was FINE in every way...

It was obvious to me that Eddie was not the least bit embarrassed about showing off his body, or his most private of parts either... From where I was standing I could also see that the guy was semi hard in the area of his cock…JEEZ…

He snickered a bit as he stood at the halfway point of the ladder… I can't tell you how sexy that hunky black guy looked standing there in the center of the ladder in just his white sweat socks… As he stood on one of the center steps he parted his feet a bit, for better balance I suppose, and I swear the crack of his ass looked like it was yawing for attention. His balls swung and my heart raced. My cock got hard in my pants and my hands were sweating and shaking a bit…

I stepped up to the ladder and gripped the sides of it to keep it steady as I climbed up onto the second step, very close to that sexy sweaty black derriere. The scent emanating from there was a bit musty yet manly at the same time. I felt really uncomfortable being directly under this guy's exposed butt, (I suppose I should have told him to get dressed and get out of my apartment but I didn't, *I couldn't…*) but it was somehow exciting at the same time. The things going through my mind were unusual but somehow familiar at the same time. I mean, I was no stranger to eating pussy…eating…

As Eddie was about to start climbing to the ceiling level of the ladder I noticed a droplet of sweat at the top of the crack of his delicious looking tight ass. Fuck, just seeing that little bead of sweat had my cock throbbing like a thing alive in my pants. As I stood there underneath that tight black ass I just knew that I had to have a taste of that droplet of sweat. It was driving me crazy. At first I was afraid but then asked myself why. Hs naked ass was in my face after all. He knew he wanted it this way; he was playing at seducing me it seemed. As Eddie was about to take another step up the ladder I climbed up closely behind him and quickly licked away that bead of forming sweat on his ass. My tongue lapped against his butt cheeks at the top of the crack and I expected him to slug me for doing what I had just done. Instead Eddie, holding tight to the sides of the ladder from where he was balanced looked down at me and grinned lecherously, as if to say, "I knew it…"

He stepped up another step, I thought why not and I did the same thing, my face close enough to that well-shaped ass to be able to smell the manly odors emanating from it. Why stop there? I took a deep breath, Eddie snickered and I saw another bead of sweat form, this time right in the center of the crack of his butt that I was falling helplessly in lust with. His crack looked so hot with a little hair showing through, and his balls dangling between his thighs was making me batty.

Eddie hadn't minded my lapping the sweat off his ass a few moments earlier so I leaned forward and did it again, more deliberately this time, really pressing my tongue against his butt cheeks and letting him feel it as I scoffed down the bead of sweat…it tasted oh so sweet I must say… I did it with one big sloppy lick…

Eddie simply faced forward, balanced on his socked feet on the ladder as I pressed my nose between his ass cheeks now, my tongue flicking and teasing him against his ass cheeks at the same time. He let out an "Ohhhhhhhhh…" sound as my tongue worked its magic…

"Hold on tight Eddie," I whispered meanly now.

I balanced myself well on the step of the ladder I was on and gripped his ass cheeks with my hands, squeezing those melons nice and tight, jiggling them a bit. The sexy black guy took a deep breath as I exposed his pink raunchy bunghole. As I said earlier I was hardly a stranger to eating pussy. Eddie's bunghole was stinking and as pink as a pussy. When I saw the little button hole back there I shook in my shoes…

"Holy fucking fuck," I whispered and stuck out my tongue.

With the very tip of my tongue I started lapping hungrily at the guy's moist and sweat dripping asshole.

"OHHHHHHHHH…" was all Eddie could say as I ate his ass chowder.

I held his ass cheeks spread apart and kissed the sides of his crack, slathering his inner bunghole with my tongue, eating his stink…

"Sorry to be taking such fucking liberties with you Eddie, but this ass of yours is sexier than a woman's I got to say," I said and I then proceeded to kiss and kiss his black ass cheeks a few times each, like a hundred times each and then plunged my tongue again into his most private crevice.

All Eddie did in response was to moan in a man's passion. The sound was deep and guttural as I ate and ate his pink hole. I spit in his hole then… He gasped as my saliva pelted his button hole and swung around a bit sexily on the ladder step. I grabbed his socked ankles and balanced him, leaning down for a moment to kiss the backs of his socked feet a few times each, sort of as a way of thanking him for this… Looking down he smiled as I kissed his socked feet, inhaling their funky odor as well…

I spit and spit into his hole, really soaking him up back there, making a nice dish for myself. Then, holding his ass cheeks spread wide I pressed my mouth against his hole and sucked, I sucked hard.

"OHHHHHHHHHH FUCKING fuck, that feels awesome," Eddie thundered as I sucked my saliva from his manhole.

It was the first words he had said since I had found him naked but for his socks on the ladder. The sounds of me slurping feverishly from the painter's asshole and his breathing in gasps and grunts filled the room…

Eddie gripped the sides of the ladder tightly, parted his legs a bit more and I was able to really get my face into his shit chute…

"AAAAAAAHHHHHHH…" he moaned, his balls dangling real low and his cock hard as steel as it pointed straight out in front of him…

What a sight we must have been on that ladder buds, the handsome black sexy painter holding on for balance as I stood balanced behind him eating his hole like it was dinner time…or lunch, seeing as it was only mid-day, har, har, har…

A few times I really gripped the guy's ass cheeks tighter than tight and held them spread wide. I wanted to see what I smelled and tasted, really see it buds. I teased Eddie by flicking the tip of my tongue around and around in his hole. I swirled my tongue in there and I swear that really got him moaning…

The heat in the room had us both sweating in no time and all it did was fuel my imagination for some more sleazy and randy fun with the guy that I had hired to paint my home office…

At that point Eddie's hole was sopped with my saliva, his ass cheeks were glistening from the way I had licked and kissed them and his muscular frame was slicked with sweat as well… I swear I wanted to eat every part of the guy at that point… As I again pressed my face into his crack and sucked hard and as he grunted and groaned I trailed three fingertips over his dangling balls. He reacted by groaning even louder so I took my next opportunity buds…

I instructed Eddie to hold on tight as I stepped down one step on the ladder…

Before he could ask what I was going to do he shrieked loudly as I inserted two fingers in his sopped hole and then began licking his dangling balls. His walls seemed to close tight around my fingers burrowing in there. I squirreled my head between his thighs and took total liberties with the guy's sweaty testicles…

"Mmm, tasty," I whispered and sucked the painter's balls alternately in and out of my mouth, applying pressure to them.

At the same time I swirled my fingers around in Eddie's ass crack. The walls of his shit chute felt warm and moist to the touch… He shrieked again as I slid a third finger in there and continued to feast on his balls…

Eddie rocked a bit on the ladder step that he was perched on and he mumbled something about the fact that he was going to shoot his load without even touching his hard cock…

I slowly slid my fingers from his hole and gripped the backs of his thighs then, holding him real tight…

I sucked the painter's balls back as far as possible with my mouth and Eddie leaned down and forward as he seemed to be holding onto the ladder for dear life at that point…

"OHHHHHHHHHH…" I heard him gurgle loudly and then he shot his load, as he said, without even touching his cock.

It sprayed out of his piss hole in torrents, splattered against the wall and dripped down in what looked like rivers…

"OHHHHHHHHHH…." Eddie groaned again and shot off two more thick ropes of semen.

The mess on the wall was sexy as all hell, and I was glad he was there to paint over it once it…once it dried up that is…

As Eddie was panting, thinking that he was done shooting his load I quickly gripped his ass cheeks, spread them wide and plastered my face back against his bunghole and licked, licked, licked…

"OHHHHHHHHH!!!!!!" Eddie swooned that time and to his shock let loose with yet another hefty discharge of painter's spunk.

It splattered on the wall with the rest of his splooge and finally, I stopped eating his ass…

As Eddie panted, heaved and gasped on his step on the ladder I gave him a few friendly swats on the rear and climbed down…

I stood there panting myself, licked my lips a few times and scoffed down Eddie's manly and musty taste that had lingered there. He looked down at me from his position on the ladder and looking up I saw his semi hard cock dangling real sexily. It was the size of a goddamned fire hose, nice and black and silky looking. A dollop of cum hung from the slit of it and I couldn't resist buds…

I leaned up and scoffed that dollop of cum off the guy's cock…

As Eddie sweated and wondered when he would start getting to paint my home office I sucked his cock hungrily…

The Fundraising Event

"RRRRMMMMMFFF!!!" was all I could say as I lay stretched out good and tight atop a huge bed of lettuce (yes you read that right, I had been turned into the centerpiece of a huge fundraiser appetizer) on a rollaway serving table.

I was naked as the day I had been born. My arms were extended over my head and my hands were tied at the wrists to the handle at the head of the rollaway table I was on. Poor me my ticklish hairy armpits were totally on display and anyone who knows me knows what the fuck that means, fucking fuck! My bare feet were elevated on a stack of cushions at the other end of the table and tied to those cushions with mounds of rope at the ankles, the rope extended from my ankles and tied around the cushions, securing said cushions to the table. My upper thighs were roped tightly together, making a nice little bed for my cum chocked danged balls to rest upon. One of my navy blue calf length nylon dress socks had become my gag. It was crammed balled up into my craw and my silk necktie had been tied over it, jamming it in place. I chewed miserably on that sock, stupidly wondering what had become of its mate, hardy fucking har and har. Gawd, every time I swallowed I was treated to a mouthful of my own foot stink.

The huge bed of lettuce (romaine, iceberg, leafy, red leafed and raw spinach) that I lay on felt cool and clammy against my naked skin and I was surrounded by shredded and chopped up purple cabbage, cut up tomatoes, sliced cucumbers, cut up raw carrots, raw sliced and diced red, green and yellow peppers, an inordinate amount of sliced pickles and all topped off with seasoned croutons. Gawd almighty, poor me, good ol' ticklish Timmy Backman had been captured again and this time I had been turned into a human hors d'oeuvre… What a way to have liberties taken with me this time out huh buds?

Looking at my sides and taking in how I was surrounded by a mess of raw salad ingredients the scent of all those danged pickles seemed to waft up at me. All I could think was, "Oh good Gawd, I really am in a pickle this time…" and rolled my eyes in my head in total disbelief over this…

Laying there naked my cock was jutted up good and rigid and stiff. As my good buddy Christopher Trevor the author would say, I was fear hard and throbbing. My juicy balls rested good and chock filled against the tops of my stretched out and tied together thighs.

"Man oh man, what an evening it's going to be," the man's voice boomed as he stood a few feet away from me, checking his reflection in the mirror as he straightened his tie. "I'll just bet we're going to raise thousands of dollars for charity tonight."

"Mmmmmmffff…" was all I could say as I looked over at the bald, handsome man, a man I knew well, a man who had had at me in my ticklish past, a man who had taken liberties with me on other occasions, he who was the emcee for the night.

"Doing okay over there laddy?" he chuckled. "Man, I can't thank you enough for volunteering for this tonight Timmy."

"RRRMMMFFFFF!!!" I grunted angrily.

I hadn't volunteered for shit! I had been sent on bank business as a representative of the company to a charity organization that called themselves "The NTC" and to bear witness to a fundraiser that they were holding in a fancy shmancy room in an exclusive and elite hotel. Winding up stripped of my suit and turned into a human hors d'oeuvre *had not* figured into my plans for the night... When I thought about my vice president at the bank, Jerry Bradshaw, and how this playful and ticklish state of affairs had originally been planned for him my skin crawled. Gawd, the whole devilish scheme had been twisted from Jerry Bradshaw to yours truly here, yours truly currently being the human salad.

"Do you have any idea how many people are out there in the audience Timmy?" the man who was nicknamed Bull asked me as he turned to me and seemed to drink in the sight of me in the tight bondage. "Why, I'll just bet we're going to make upwards of a million dollars tonight..."

"GGGRRRRRFFFF!!!!" I railed.

"It could happen you know," Bull said, sounding totally enthusiastic. "We've made nearly a million dollars in the past, nearly, but not quite. With you here tonight as a volunteer I'm sure we'll make it... And not to mention it, but I will anyway, there are some pretty wealthy people out there, so I'm sure they'll fork it over..."

He stepped over to the table, dapper in his charcoal colored business suit. Grinning down at me he plucked a piece of raw pepper off the table and popped it into his mouth. He chewed it, looking down at me as I lay there totally helpless. When he squeezed one of my nipples my hard cock oozed a dollop of pre cum...

"RULL, remme ree," I said, trying to say, "Let me free..."

As the man nicknamed Bull leered down at me my mind wandered back to how I had come to be tied to a table as the centerpiece of a huge salad…

My name, as you well know by now is Timothy Backman… It was on a recent Friday afternoon when my vice president, Jerry Bradshaw, at the bank I work for had summoned me to his office to tell me about the charity organization that our company was going to sponsor. Actually, the bank was going to sponsor one of the organizations charitable fund raising events in exchange for some free advertising in their monthly newsletter and on their website. It would be really good pr for the bank. Mr. Bradshaw's Secretary Janice had called me on my private line and said that the VP wanted to see me post-haste. I looked at my watch, saw that it was just about quitting time, took a deep breath, smiled, and told Janice that I would be in Jerry's office post-haste. I quickly straightened my tie, climbed into my light gray suit jacket and walked at a rather quick pace to the vice president's office…

When I got to the reception area Janice looked up from her desk, smiled real big at me (somehow, and not to sound all that vain, but I always had the feeling that Janice has a crush on me) and told me to go right in. I thanked her, stepped to Jerry Bradshaw's door, knocked politely and entered.

"Hey Tim, come on in man, close the door, this won't take long," Jerry said as he waved me in from behind his huge desk. "Have a seat…"

"Thanks Jerry," I said and sat down opposite him at his desk.

Jerry is a ruggedly handsome guy in his early fifties, although with the way he keeps himself in shape most people think he's in his mid forties. He has salt and pepper colored hair, piercing blue eyes and stands nearly six feet tall in his musculature. I've heard it rumored at the bank how women have said that if they were his wife they would not leave him alone at night… Actually, I'd heard it rumored that some of the men at the bank felt the same way about handsome Jerry Bradshaw.

"Ready for the weekend?" he asked me, making some small talk as he riffled through some papers, obviously looking for something he wanted me to see.

"As ready as ever," I replied and rested a foot on one knee.

"The wife and I are headed upstate for the weekend," Jerry said. "Just the two of us, we're leaving the kids with my mother… As you know we have a small place up there…"

"Sounds good…" I said, not really caring one way or the other. "Stephanie and I are probably just going to relax most of the weekend. I know she wants to take Tim junior to see that new Disney film that just opened, so that's more than likely what I'll be doing…"

"That sounds nice…" Jerry said.

Jerry found the paper he was looking for and held it up, looking at it as he spoke…

"Tell me Tim, have you ever heard of an organization called "The NTC?" the VP asked me.

"Hmm, can't say that I have," I replied and gripped my socked ankle as it lay on my knee. "What kind of an organization is it?"

"They're a charity Tim," Jerry said. "They're having their annual fund raiser next week and they've approached the bank for a donation…"

I grinned and asked, "So how much are we going to get as a tax write-off?"

"Good one Tim, very good," Jerry laughed and reached across the desk to hand me the paper he was holding."

I quickly skimmed over what was printed on the paper…

"NTC Annual Fund Raiser, Ages eighteen and up all welcome, Wednesday, September 7th, festivities begin at 7:30 PM till 12:30 AM, the "Imperial Room at the Grand Diamond Hotel on forty-Fifth Street between Broadway and seventh Avenue…Dinner and drinks will be served…" I murmured and then looked up at Jerry, my eyes ago ogle. "Whoa, the Imperial Room at the Grand Diamond? Holy crow Jerry, that room holds up to about two hundred people or so, and it comes equipped with a stage and all… Celebrity weddings have taken place in that room…"

"I know," Jerry Bradshaw said, looking at me intently now. "This is why the bank can't refuse their request for a donation. It sounds like they're a pretty hefty and top of the line organization. If we refused their request it wouldn't look good for us. Now, in return for the donation the NTC organization has agreed to advertise our company in their monthly newsletter for the next year and to give us a plug on their website as well…"

"That sounds great," I said. "Where do I come in?"

"Well, I want you to go to the fundraising dinner as a representative of the bank," Jerry said.

I pursed my lips together and shook my head in the affirmative…

"Sure thing Jerry," I said and put my foot back down on the floor. "I mean, the Imperial Room at the Grand Diamond hotel? I wouldn't turn that down…"

"Good, good deal Tim," Jerry said. "Now, as you know the fundraiser is on Wednesday night. On Monday night I'd like you to go to the organization's main office and meet with their CEO, Frank Brucco… Mr. Brucco is actually the gentleman who called and requested the donation from the bank in exchange for the free advertising they'll give us. He said he called me because he had seen my picture in one of the business columns in one of the newspapers where the bank was mentioned. He also said how he would have liked me to come to the fund raiser, but you know my schedule Tim."

"Yeah, I sure do Jerry…" I replied.

As he spoke Jerry handed me another paper…

"That's the address of their home office in the Chelsea area," Jerry said as I looked at the second paper.

It was actually a flyer that advertised the "NTC" organization and gave the address of where their home office was, in the Chelsea area of Manhattan. Their logo was a pair of open palmed hands, the fingers and thumbs slightly bent inwardly. At the sight of that logo I felt a slight chill crawl up my spine, although I didn't register the feeling with my ever-loving weakness at that moment.

"Hmm, NTC, You're in Good Hands with us," I read the slogan under the picture of the hands. "Located at Five Sixteen, Sixteenth Street, suites one and two. If you ask me it sounds like some kind of insurance company Jerry."

"Well, whatever kind of organization they are the bank is sponsoring this fund raiser of theirs Tim," Jerry said. "So on Monday night after work go to their main office to meet with their CEO…"

"Mr. Frank Brucco," I said.

"Yep, that's the man," Jerry said with a smile. "I'll have my secretary set up the appointment with him for you. I already told Mr. Frank Brucco that I would make sure that someone from the bank covers their event…"

"Thanks Jerry, anything in particular you want me to find out from Mr. Brucco?" I asked.

"Just the usual crap about these charity organizations, what kind of a business they are, how much of a donation are they expecting the bank to make…" Jerry said and grinned.

"I get it Jerry, consider it done," I said and folded up both sheets of paper he had given me, sliding them into the side pocket of my suit jacket. "Say, could I bring Stephanie to the fund raiser at the Grand Diamond hotel on Wednesday?"

"I don't think so Tim," Jerry said apologetically. "It's nothing personal mind you, just that this is strictly business and the bank did agree to send just one person as a representative…"

"I understand, I understand totally," I said.

"Okay, then you're all set," Jerry said. "Meet with Mr. Frank Brucco on Monday night, get him to answer some questions and then get back to me on Tuesday either by phone or here in my office…"

"Will do," I said getting to my feet and holding out my hand. "Thanks for the assignment Jerry. I'm sure it'll be a night to remember…"

I shook hands with my boss and I could not have imagined the irony of my words at that moment…

As I thought about that afternoon in my bosses office my mind returned to the present and I watched, tied to that danged table as two beautiful women of the "NTC" organization were putting the finishing touches on the salad that I was the centerpiece of. To be totally exact here they were adding radishes to the salad, actually they were surrounding my tied up bare feet with those radishes, really putting my sexy tootsies on display for the upcoming festivities. Bull had taken my sock gag out of my mouth before leaving me with the two dollies and their radishes, telling me had to go out to the main festivity room and check on some last minute stuff before he wheeled me out on the stage. Looking up at the two beautiful and curvaceous women my cock twitched like a thing alive in it's erect state and I pleaded with Bull to untie me, to let me go, telling him again that I was here on official business from the bank I work for…

"Of course you're here on official business, that's why I set you up the way I got you there…" Bull laughed and stuck my navy blue sock that had been my gag into his suit jacket pocket. "I want you to see firsthand and right up front just what our organization does and what it's all about…"

That said Bull left the room, leaving me in the care of the two sexy women and their boxes of red, red radishes… Smiling down at me they took position at either side of the table at my bound up feet. They introduced themselves to me as Margo and Deborah. I pursed my lips, rolled my eyes in disbelief again over all this and sarcastically said, "Nice to meet you ladies, I'm Tim Backman. I would shake hands with each of you but as you can see I'm a little tied up at the moment…hardy har and har…"

The two women giggled stupidly and went to work surrounding my bare feet with the radishes. Margo was about five feet ten inches tall. She had silky black hair, shoulder length and dark sinister looking eyes. Her chest was huge and I swear she had tits ala Pamela Anderson. I managed to steal a glance down at the floor and saw that with her miniskirt outfit she was sporting patent leather high heeled pumps with black nylon stockings. My head spun at the sight of Margo's curvy feet in those shoes and my hard cock lifted itself from my thighs and pointed straight up at the ceiling, Gawd!

"It's nice to meet you as well Mr. Backman," Margo said, looking hungrily at my throbbing hardness as it seemed to pledge allegiance to her and Deborah. "He sure is a big boy wouldn't you say?"

"He sure is," Deborah said her also looking at my cock like she wanted to devour it whole. "He sure is a big boy…"

Deborah was slightly taller than Margo. She had blond hair

with brown roots showing, obviously a dye job. Her eyes were brown and like Margo she was clad in a sexy miniskirt type of outfit. Her tits were practically hanging out of her skimpy top. Unlike Margo though Deborah sported knee high red leather boots, but you wouldn't hear me complaining about that. My cock remained at its kickstand position as the ladies did their work and teased me mercilessly…

"Uh ladies, girls, could I speak to you two please?" I asked them, grinning stupidly like a teenaged schoolboy.

"Sure, we can talk and radish your feet at the same time…" Deborah said, tweaking one of my toes and giggling. "Oops, I meant to say ravish your feet…"

"Uh yeah, that's what I'm trying to avoid here," I said, trying to muster up some authority into my voice. "Now look, when I said that I was here on bank business I meant it. Mr. Brucco, Bull, Bull and his cohorts managed to trick and shanghai me into the position you see me in here. I'm really not supposed to be a human salad ladies."

As I spoke they held their boxes of radishes in one hand each and spread radishes around and around my feet with their other hands…

"So if you ladies would untie me I'll gladly get dressed in my suit and take a seat out there in the audience and…" I began.

"That won't work Mr. Backman," Margo said, her sounding more like a dominatrix as she spoke, whereas Deborah sounded like a goddamned dumb blond.

"And why won't it work Margo?" I asked her through clenched teeth.

"Because Bull has one of your socks," she laughed. "Your suit would be incomplete…"

I leaned my head back and felt a wave of helplessness engulf me as both women meanly trailed a long, sharp fingernail each up the bottom of one of my bare feet each. They started at the heels of my feet and inched their way upwards…

"OOOOOOOOO, ha, ha, ha, ha, ha, ha, d-don't do that, don't tickle my feet!" I laughed, at the same time knowing that I would get no help from these two foxy ladies. "J-just do what you're being paid to do and spread those radishes…"

"Paid?" Margo asked. "Why Mr. Backman, we're not getting paid, like you we're all volunteers here…"

They finger-nailed the bottoms of my feet again…harder this time…

"HOOOOOOOO, ha, ha, ha, ha, ha, I-I am not a volunteer here," I cackled. "I-I've been had is what happened to me… HOO, HOO, HOO, HOO, HOO, HOO, HOO!!!!!!"

"He sounds so cute when he laughs…" Deborah snickered and stepped to the center of the table, looking down at my cock as its one eye looked up at her.

The two women set their boxes of radishes down for the moment…

I gulped hard and in disbelief as Deborah opened her mouth, leaned down and slurped my hard muscle pipe into her velvety feeling mouth. Her glistening saliva mixed with her red lipstick and she slithered her mouth downward and around the crown and shaft of my erect maleness. Margo pressed my big toes together and suckled them into her mouth at the same time…

"OHHHHRRRRR fucking fucks, I'm a married guy…" I grunted as chills and thrills coursed through my very being.

As the ladies sucked my cock and my big toes they tickled

my balls and the bottoms of my feet at the same time… I laughed and hemmed and hawed in ecstasy…

My mind wandered back in time to the meeting in Bull, er, Mr. Frank Brucco's office that past Monday…

"Can I help you Sir?" the twenty something handsome young man at the reception desk asked me as I stepped off the elevator at the offices of "NTC."

The walls of the reception area were adorned with pictures of the organization's logo, those open palmed hands with the bent fingers. I have to admit that since the meeting in Jerry Bradshaw's office when he'd shown me the picture of those hands the image had for some reason haunted me all weekend…

"Uh yes, I'm here to see Mr. Frank Brucco," I said, stepping up to the reception desk, me clad in a brown suit, a light blue brown striped shirt with matching tie and slip-on brown dress shoes and with my hand extended. "I'm Tim Backman from the bank. Mr. Brucco is expecting me I believe…"

"Ah yes, Mr. Backman, very nice to see you," the male receptionist said and reached up to shake hands with me.

He had a grip like iron and pumped my hand till I thought I would be hefted right out of my shoes…

"Mr. Brucco is indeed expecting you," he said, let go of my hand and reached for the phone on his desk.

He dialed three digits and then said, "Yes Mr. Brucco, Mr. Backman is here…"

He paused to listen for a few seconds, looked up at me and said softly, "You can go right in" as he pointed to the door to Mr. Brucco's office.

"Thank you very much," I said with a smile and stepped over to Brucco's door.

I knuckle knocked twice and heard a very deep voice call out, "It's open, come on in…"

I stepped into Mr. Brucco's office, closing the door behind me…

"Mr. Brucco, I'm Tim Backman," I said, entering his office and approaching the big man who was standing behind his desk with my palm outstretched.

"Ah yes, Backman, Tim Backman, very good to meet you my boy," Frank Brucco thundered at me, a wide smile on his wire rimmed spectacled face. "Jerry Bradshaw at the bank called me himself to arrange our little teat a teat here…"

"Our uh, teat a teat Sir?" I asked him as he gripped my hand solidly, just as solidly as the receptionist had, pumping it, and me, up and down.

"Our meeting, the talk we're going to have you and me, our upcoming conversation, our chat, our teat a teat," he laughed as he went on pumping my hand.

"Oh, I see," I laughed as well.

Somehow he looked familiar but for some reason I could not exactly place him… He was dressed in a black suit with a white shirt and a black and white striped silk tie, very New York, very fashionable looking. He appeared to be extremely muscular, what with the way his upper arms and chest bulged in his suit that is and he was as bald as an eagle, his head as shiny as a diamond.

"Have a seat Mr. Backman," he said, letting go of my hand and sitting down in his chair.

“Thank you Mr. Brucco, thank you very much,” I said and sat down opposite him at his desk.

His wire rim spectacles were the very old fashioned style, sort of like what the dapper dandy’s back in the roaring twenties wore. They made his eyes look almost bug-eyed.

“Now, what can I do for you lad, er- Mr. Backman,” Frank Brucco asked me.

“Well,” I began and crossed one leg over the other, making my foot dangle a few inches off the floor. “My Vice President at the bank, Jerry Bradshaw asked me to be a representative of our company at your fundraiser this Wednesday night.”

“Ah yes, Jerry Bradshaw,” Frank Brucco said, sounding almost dreamy as he clasped his hands in front of him and glanced up at the ceiling. “We here were hoping that *he* would be able to make the fundraiser as well. That’s one good lookin’ so and so that you work for Mr. Backman…”

“Well uh, I’ll be sure to tell Mr. Bradshaw you said that Mr. Brucco, I’m sure he’ll appreciate it,” I said. “Where uh, where did you learn of Jerry Bradshaw?”

“His picture ran alongside an article in the Wall Street Daily, the article was about computers, the internet and how both are affecting today’s banking world,” Brucco said, just as Jerry had figured. “He sure had a lot of interesting things to say…sure wish he could make it on Wednesday night…”

“Well, he would love to have come Mr. Brucco,” I said. “But as a first VP of the bank he has many, many responsibilities, you understand…”

As I spoke I lifted my leg higher and rested my brown socked ankle on my knee.

"Of course I understand Mr. Backman, and I'm not all that disappointed at all," Frank Brucco said and almost leered lustfully at me, another thing about him that seemed familiar somehow. "After all he sent us you, his handsome boy wonder…"

I must have turned three different shades of red in the face as I said, "Well thank you Mr. Brucco…"

"I, I mean, we, *we* at the bank were wondering how much of a donation your organization was expecting from us, from the bank," I said, giving my tie a tug.

"That's entirely up to you and your Mr. Bradshaw," Brucco said, his palms open in front of him. "What were you planning on offering?"

"Well, seeing as your company plans to advertise the bank in its monthly newsletter and you plan to give us a plug on your website we figured around this much," I said and handed Mr. Brucco a slip of paper that had been in my suit jacket pocket.

He unfolded the paper and his eyebrows rose nearly as high as his forehead…

"Well, well, all this plus a handsome representative from the bank," he said and pointed at me.

Again I blushed red, said, "Thank you, I admire your outspokenness and your candor Mr. Brucco…"

"I'm glad Backman, it's that outspokenness that's gotten me where I am at this point in my life and with the charity I run here," he said with an air of authority.

"What does your charity do with the money it collects Mr. Brucco?" I asked him and gripped my ankle.

"We help the homeless; we help families that have been affected by things like teenage drug use, teen pregnancy, that sort of thing…" he replied. "We send food to war ravaged countries…"

"Sounds very noble if I do say so myself," I said. "I have a young son and I'm glad that there are organizations like yours out here Mr. Brucco…"

"So am I Mr. Backman," Frank Brucco said, getting to his feet. "Now then, if that's all for the moment…"

"Oh sure, sure, I don't want to take up anymore of your time than necessary," I said, I also getting to my feet, my hand outstretched.

"It's not that at all Mr. Backman, you seem like a nice enough sort of guy," he chuckled as he reached for my hand and gripped it tight. "It's just that I have much to do before Wednesday night."

"Of course," I said as he pumped my hand. "So I'll see you at 7:30 on Wednesday night in the Imperial room at the Grand Diamond hotel…"

"You can feel free to arrive even before 7:30 lad, er- Mr. Backman," Frank Brucco said as he let go of my hand. "We'll, *me,* me and my associates, we'll be there getting everything ready starting around sixish or so…if you get there early it'll be no problem whatsoever, in fact I can promise you an eventful evening…"

"Well thank you Mr. Brucco, I think I'll accept that offer…" I said, not knowing the hell I was plunging myself into yet again. "Six o'clock it is…"

"See you then Mr. Backman…" Frank Brucco said as I smiled and politely saw myself out of his office.

"Oh, and I'll tell Mr. Bradshaw that you're disappointed that he can't come to the fundraising event…" I said, my head poking in the door for a last moment, still trying to figure out where I knew Frank

Brucco from.

"Thanks Mr. Backman, but also tell him thanks for sending his boy wonder in his stead…" Frank Brucco replied.

On the train ride home I realized that I had forgotten to ask Frank Brucco what the letters "NTC" stood for in the name of his organization… I figured it was no big deal and that I would find out Wednesday night. Oh man, how right I was, I would certainly find out buds…

After Margo and Deborah had finished surrounding my bare feet with the radishes and after they had finished teasing and tickling me they left the room where Bull had me tied to a table in the form of a human salad. They had sucked my cock a few times each but had not let me get to the point of no return. So my poor cock was hard and throbbing even more-so now… The ladies had left remnants of their lipstick and saliva on my shaft and I stupidly thought how I would have to clean that off before I got home that night… Bull returned a scant few seconds after the two women had left the room…

"Okay laddy, everything out there in the Imperial room is good to go, we're all set," Bull said, stepping over to the table I was tied to. "Now to just make the last arrangements on you and I'll wheel you out there…"

"Oh Gawd, oh Good Gawd Bull, no, no, don't do this," I began as Bull reached into his suit jacket for my navy blue sock. "Please man; don't bring me out there in front of all those people…MMMFFFFFF…"

My eyes rolled in my head as Bull again gagged me with my danged sock, cramming the saliva soaked thing in my craw, tying my silk necktie over it as well, jamming it firmly back in my mouth…

"Okay laddy, here's what's going to happen when I get you out there," Bull said, laying things like feathers, sprigs of pine needles and swizzle sticks around my naked and trussed up salad surrounded body.

"I'm goin' to wheel you around the entire room so that all our benefactors and members can get a good look at you…then when we stop at each table I'm going to allow ticklers who want to tickle you to do so. They can use their fingers if they want or they can use the supplies I just laid out on your table… Of course they'll have to make a donation first. After that they get to tickle your body part of their choice…"

"RRRRRFFFF…" I grunted as Bull took up position at the side of the table.

"Looks like you're ready for your first "National Ticklers Convention" fundraiser my laddy," Bull laughed and clipped a cock ring around the base of my cock and balls, just to keep me good and rigidly stiff and on the infernal brink.

The next thing I knew I was being wheeled toward the door that led to the "Imperial Room…"

"RFFFFFFF…" I said one last time and Bull took the sock out of my mouth… "B-Bull, I beg of you man, don't take me out there like this all naked and worked up in the cock like I am!!"

"Ah Timmy me laddy, you act as though the people who belong to the "NTC" organization never saw a naked guy tied up with an erection before…" Bull laughed and wheeled me toward the Imperial Room…

I'm sure you're wondering as you read this how I went from being a representative from the bank for the fundraiser to being the main attraction if you would. Well, sadly for ticklish ol' me Timmy Backman, everyone's favorite ticklish buddy, (everyone meaning my buddy Ronald, my rival for my wife's affections Valerie, Valerie's boy toy Douglas, my buddy Jim, and of course I hate to say it but my ever conniving brother Bruce and even my dear wife Stephanie) it's a sad old and usual (unusual?) tale…

After my meeting with Mr. Frank Brucco on Monday evening in his office I reported back to Jerry Bradshaw on Tuesday. At that time I still didn't know that Frank Brucco was Bull so I was still very excited about the upcoming event on Wednesday night. I told Jerry about my quick but productive meeting with the head of the "NTC" and that everything was set for Wednesday night.

"Sounds good Tim, you did well as usual," Jerry said to me. "I suggest you have a good time at the fundraiser."

"Thanks Jerry," I replied, shaking hands with him. "And thank you again for the assignment."

"Sure thing man, sure thing" Jerry said.

"Oh, and Mr. Brucco said how they had really been hoping that you would have made the fundraiser," I said and Jerry stopped pumping my hand and just held it tight. "But I explained how you're a busy man and all…"

"Hmm, he said that huh?" Jerry asked with a grin.

"Yeah, he had seen your picture in the Wall Street Daily…just like you had suspected…" I said and decided not to say anymore at that point.

The way Jerry was still holding onto my hand made me wonder just how much I should say about Mr. Frank Brucco's supposed fascination with my handsome vice president.

"Well, anyway Tim, you have a good time tomorrow night at the "NTC" fundraiser…" Jerry said and released his grip on my hand.

"I will Jerry, I certainly will," I said with a smile.

As Bull wheeled me out of the room where I had been made into a human salad I thought about that last conversation with Jerry and thought how if he only knew what had now become of me…

I had arrived at the Grand Diamond hotel at six PM on the dot, just as Frank Brucco had requested of me. I made my way to the Imperial Room and saw that some of Mr. Brucco's associates were busy setting up tables, placing chairs around the tables, setting up microphones on the stage and just bustling all over the place it seemed. For some strange reason some of the guys looked really familiar, just as Mr. Brucco had, but again for that same strange reason I could not place them. I saw their "NTC" logo in frames adorning the walls and as I stood there clad very sharply in a Brooks Brother's navy blue suit, starched white shirt, a burgundy silk tie, highly shined black lace-up wingtips and suspenders one of the guys came over to me.

"Mr. Backman right?" he asked me. "Mr. Timothy Backman from the bank?"

"Yeah, that would be me," I said as the guy looked me over in my Wall Street attire, he wearing worn jeans, work boots and a tee shirt.

I supposed that coming early to the event in a business suit did kind of single me out and that was how he knew who I was.

"Mr. Brucco is waiting for you in the back room Sir," he said, pointing at a door at the far end of the exquisite Imperial Room.

"Waiting for me?" I asked.

"Yeah, he said you could meet him in there," the muscular guy said to me. "No need for you to be out here while we get things all set up…"

"Uh sure, thanks," I said and walked toward the door that the guy had just indicated.

When I got to the door I knocked twice and I heard Frank Brucco's voice call out, "Yeah, who is it?"

"Uh, it's Tim Backman, Tim Backman from the bank Mr. Brucco," I called out.

"Ah good, you're just in time for a salad appetizer," I heard Brucco call out. "Come on in Tim!"

I walked into the room and saw that Frank Brucco was standing with his back to me at a large rollaway table. Three other men were in the room as well. Mr. Brucco was dressed like I was in a suit, his being charcoal gray. The three guys standing around the table with him were all dressed like the guy who had just directed me to this room, jeans, work boots and tee shirts…

"So glad you could come early Timmy me laddy," Mr. Brucco said as I approached the table.

"Y-your laddy?" I asked and suddenly my heart thundered in my chest. "Wh-why did you just call me that Mr. Brucco?"

Frank Brucco turned from the table he was standing in front of and looked at me straight on. He wasn't wearing his glasses. I gulped hard. I still hadn't taken in the fact that the tabletop was literally covered and swathed in lettuce.

"Holy crow, Bull!!" I blurted out. "Y-you're Bull, from the leather bar!!"

"Glad you recognized me this time laddy," Bull said in that baritone sounding voice of his. "I was wondering if you had recognized me in my office the other day and maybe, just maybe, because of that you wouldn't show up here after all…Amazing how a pair of glasses can mask another's identity don't you think? Sort of like Clark Kent and Superman if you would…"

"B-but you're a bartender…" I said, not understanding this at all.

As Bull and I spoke the three muscular guys in the room with him were slowly surrounding me, wedging me in so to speak…actually it was eerily reminiscent of how they had crowded me in and snagged me at the leather bar…

"My buddy owns that leather bar where you and I had the pleasure of meeting," Bull said, reaching out and tweaking the knot in my tie. "I sometimes tend bar for him there just to help him out when he's short on staff. Running the "NTC" is what I do full time… My name really is Frank Brucco but my nickname is Bull…"

"NTC…" I said wonderingly. "Tell me Mr. Brucco, I mean Bull, what do the letters NTC stand for?"

Before replying Bull and his three cohorts in the room with me laughed loudly and raucously.

"What the hell is so funny?" I asked, trying to sound as angry and annoyed as possible over being tricked.

"Oh, you're going to love this me laddy, with you being a tickle fetishist and all…" Bull cackled, his fingers moving down my tie as he laughed and talked.

"I-I am not a tickle fetishist, I've for some reason always been a tickle *victim*…" I said, not believing the words that were spewing from my mouth.

Bull and his three buddies laughed louder…

"A tickle victim, a tickle fetishist victim is more appropriate I would say laddy," Bull said in a thundering tone.

My heart was beyond pounding now…

"NTC" stands for National Ticklers Convention…" Bull said and let go of my tie.

Needless to say I was dumbfounded. Fucking fuck, with the picture of the open palmed hands with the bent fingers as their logo I should have known that the organization had something to do with tickling.

“ National Ticklers, NATIONAL TICKLERS CONVENTION?” I rasped. “Holy fucking fucks Bull. You mean to tell me that your “NTC” organization has approached a corporate domain, a bank for a donation?”

“Sure thing laddy, and look who they sent me,” Bull laughed. “Is this fate or what? I suppose you could look at this as the sequel of your time at the leather bar…”

“Oh no, no, no fucking way Bull,” I said, slowly backing away from him, shaking in my wingtips. “There is no way, *no way at all*, that I’m going to participate in any ticklish scenarios…”

“But Timmy me laddy, you’re the bank representative after all,” Bull said, reached out and grabbed my tie again. “And we’ve already prepared the salad table…”

That said Bull yanked me forward by my tie, using it as a leash of sorts… He held my tie tight by the center of it, pulled it upward and then spun me round and round a few times, dancing me in my wingtips as he did so…

“H-hey, st-stop this now!!” I sputtered, having been taken by surprise, my arms flailing at my sides and trying to reach for something to grab onto.

Bull then let go of my tie and sent me spiraling a bit forward…

I stumbled stupidly forward and was then standing in front of the large rollaway table that had been covered in layers upon layers of all sorts of lettuce…

"OOFFF, hey, take it easy man," I grunted, and as soon as I got my balance straightened out my tie.

I looked down at the table covered in lettuce and Bull stepped to the other side of it, his three cohorts crowded in around me from behind… The scent of raw lettuce wafted up at me…

"What is this Bull?" I asked. "What does this have to do with a national ticklers convention? It looks like a mess of lettuce all over a serving table of some sort…"

"Exactly my laddy, my handsome boy wonder executive," Bull said. "And guess, *just guess* what we plan to use as the centerpiece for this over-sized salad?"

I didn't need to guess… I gulped hard, turned on my heel to head out the door of the room, but as I did so one of Bull's cohorts grabbed my upper arms and held me tight…

"H-hey, what do you think you're up to muscle boy?" I asked sarcastically.

The muscle guy got a grip on me at the arms and then started spinning me round and round and round in a clockwise direction.

"H-HEY, now stop this, stop this foolishness now!!" I garbled as I spun, seeing my tie sailing out in front of me as I was again danced around the room.

Every time I tried to make my way away from the overly muscular guy he was again able to grab me and send me propelling, spinning me till the room was spinning in my vision…

"B-Bull, I-I'm getting all dizzied here…" I said angrily, my arms bent outward in front of me now.

"That is the idea me laddy," I heard Bull say as his cohort did the dirty work of spinning me like a top.

The muscle guy tossed me on rickety and unbalanced feet over to his buddy and he proceeded to spin me counter clockwise…

"Oh jeez, th-this is just like the night Ronald snagged me in my bathroom at home…" I murmured as the two men had their fun with me…

I was in spin-around hell as the two men tossed me back and forth between themselves, one of them spinning me clockwise and the other spinning me counter clockwise. It sure befuddled my brain what they were doing and it also gave them the advantage they would need when the time came to de-suit me. The third guy took his turn at spinning me by hoisting me above his huge, broadly muscular shoulders and began rotating me with his hands like I was tethered to a spiral bit of some sort.

"AWWWWHHHHH jeez Bull…" I cawed as I was airplane spun. "Tell your muscle stack here to put me down huh?

I was looking at the ceiling as the guy spun me and spun me…

When he'd had enough of showing me the ceiling he tossed me upwards and as I came spinning down he caught me from the front this time.

"And here we go again Mr. Laddy," the guy laughed and spun me again above his shoulders, this time as I was facing the floor.

When he'd had enough of airplane spinning me he put me down on the floor and his two buddies took over once more, dancing me across the floor as they spun me clockwise and counter clockwise. At that point I could barely focus anymore…

"Okay boys that should be enough for now…" Bull called out a short while later.

The two men let go of me and sent me wobbling back to the side of the salad table. Before I could stumble onto the mess of lettuce they each grabbed me from behind.

"No, no…" I garbled as they hoisted me a few inches off the floor…

"Now Timmy, now you see why I wanted you here early and before the festivities started…" Bull laughed, coming back around the table and standing in front of me as I dangled a few inches off the floor, my head spinning in a two direction orbit of sorts.

"Bull, call off your lackeys," I seethed. "This is not the leather bar and I do not intend to be tickle tortured here at your so called fundraiser…"

"We'll see about that Timmy me laddy, we'll just see," Bull said and looked at his third cohort.

Together, Bull and his three lackeys worked quickly in de-suiting me…

"NO, NO," I shouted as my jacket and tie were stripped off me.

Bull made a real show of snapping my suspenders in the back as two of his cronies got my suit trousers off me… Being that I had been dizzied into near oblivion there wasn't much I could do to stop the men as they worked at getting my clothes off me…

A short while later, my clothes stashed in a storage chest, except for one of my socks and my tie that is I found myself again lifted off the floor by Bull's three buddies. Two of them had me by my upper body and one of them held my bared ankles real tight. I was in a prone position as the three men held me directly next to the lettuce covered table. My hands were bound tight in front of me and my feet were tied as well. Fucking fucks, I was naked as the day I had been born…

"Bull, Jerry Bradshaw will hear of this man, he'll get you for this!" I squawked as the three men held me over the huge bed of lettuce.

"The real question here me laddy is actually, will Jerry Bradshaw get you?" Bull asked me. "You see, I plan on holding onto you for the entire evening. There's no chance whatsoever of you calling him to get you out of this..."

That said Bull gave the bottom of one of my bared feet a quick scribble tickle... I laughed loudly and then Bull instructed his three brood's men to get me secured to the salad topped table, indicating that they still had a lot of work ahead of them before the fund raiser began...

I gasped at the clammy and cold feeling of the lettuce on my back and thighs as I was set down on the table and stretched out...

"Comfortable *laddy*?" one of Bull's cohorts asked me teasingly.

"F-fuckers..." I grumbled, my head still spinning a tad as they propped my feet atop a stack of cushions, yanked my arms up above me and went to work tying me to the tabletop...

While Bull proceeded to work with his people in preparing the Imperial Room I was turned into a human salad...

And there you have it, what was the outset for what would turn out to be a dreaded and ticklish fundraiser for your favorite laddy here...

Bull wheeled me down a short hallway and then into the "Imperial Room" proper...

"Ladies and Gentlemen of the "NTC"," the announcer who was presently onstage announced into the microphone. "For your viewing and ticklish pleasure our host for the evening "Mr. Frank Brucco" and his ticklish laddy, “Tim.”

Bull left me in the epicenter of the room as he walked up onstage and stood where the announcer had just been standing… I looked around desperately, feeling totally mortified and totally on display. To my horror I saw people aiming cameras and camcorders at me. FUCKING FUCKS!! I saw the two women who had surrounded my feet with radishes and sucked my cock and tickled me. They waved over at me, licking their lips as they did so. Looking at them with my mouth agape I stole a glance at my ringed cock and saw traces of their lipstick still there. I looked back at them all a gaga. I saw a lot of familiar faces that I now remembered from the leather bar. Gawd almighty but I was tied up and naked in front of all these people… I saw straight couples, gay couples, tables with mixed couples…GAWD!!!

“Good evening ladies and gentlemen of the “NTC” or to be more precise, the National Tickler’s Convention,” I heard Bull’s voice as it boomed over the crowd from the microphone set up onstage.

I turned my attention to the host of the evening, my eyes throwing imaginary daggers at him…

“For this year’s fundraiser I’ve managed to bring us a very special added attraction,” Bull said, pointing over at me. “A true blue banker boy, ladies and gentlemen I give you my special ticklish laddy, Tim!”

A round of applause erupted and as I squirmed atop the salad table my hard cock pointed straight up again. My tied balls ached and churned… I thanked God for small favors wherein Bull hadn’t announced my last name…jeez…

“The first round of tonight’s events will be a collection of small donations ladies and gentlemen,” Bull went on. “Tim is our appetizer for the evening, as you can see.”

A smattering of laughter ensued for a few moments from the

audience…

“Later on he’ll be our main course as well…” Bull chuckled. “And of course our dessert…”

Again the audience laughed at Bull’s lame monologue…

“Being that as it is I will soon wheel Tim around to all of your tables,” Bull said. “While Tim is at your table you will be free to perform some ticklish endeavors on him. You may use your hands and fingers or you may use some of the items set out on my laddy’s salad table. The choice will be yours ladies and gentlemen...please feel free to take liberties. Before you get to tickle Tim though you will be asked for a small donation to our “NTC.”

As Bull spoke I saw women reaching for their purses and men reaching for their wallets… Gawd, I was about to go to Tickle Hell in a hand basket… I lifted my head and looked around, quickly counting the tables. There were ten tables in all, ten people at each table. Gawds almighty, that meant that one hundred people were going to be tickling me that night! I looked around a tad more and realized that besides the one hundred people at the tables there were numerous waiters. Ha, waiters my ticklish feet, they were Bull’s pals from the leather bar cleverly tuxedoed as waiters… One of the waiters silently stepped over to the salad table I was trussed to, placed the palm of his hand over my forehead and gently pressed it downward.

“Head down laddy,” the waiter said softly and laughingly popped a slice of tomato into my mouth.

I chewed angrily…

“For your donation you will be permitted to tickle any body part on Timmy that you choose, for as long as five minutes,” Bull went on and I squirmed miserably at his words.

“Any body part that is, except his cock or balls. As you can see my handsome laddy is balanced on the edge and for our ticklish purposes tonight that's just the way we want him to stay… When I start the bidding auction is when Timmy's most cherished parts will be up for ticklish grabs."

The audience members made some slight sounds of disappointment over the fact that they would not be allowed to tickle my cock and balls till much later… I took a deep breath and my eyes again shot imaginary daggers at Bull, my captor for this evening of ticklish trials… The waiter standing next to my table kept his hand on my forehead to prevent me from looking around anymore. I chewed despondently on the slice of tomato he had popped into my mouth and swallowed it…

Bull finished his opening monologue of announcements, handed the microphone back over to the guy who had introduced him and made his way back over to me.

"Let the festivities begin!" the announcer cackled into the microphone as Bull wheeled me toward table number one.

The first table, as all the tables, had ten occupants, all seated in a circle. There were three men and seven women. The seven women were all curvaceous and sexy. My cock throbbed and drooled. I pursed my lips together in the horror to come. I didn't speak a word, seeing as I figured I was going to need my strength for all the laughing I was going to be doing…

Tickling the Greatest Baseball Player in the World

“It was an awesome game huh guys?” I asked my two buddies and CO-workers as we stood around a bench in the locker room of the world’s most famous baseball team. “I couldn’t believe it how the world’s greatest player hit that homerun when they were down to just seconds and won the game for them.

“Yeah, it was pretty amazing,” Chris said, looking downward at the bench and leering lecherously. “I bet the stud was really sweating in his socks, as I like to say…”

We’re groundskeeper’s for the stadium. We keep the stadium looking spiffy and presentable. We even kept the world’s greatest baseball team’s locker room in tip-top shape for them. Without us the members of the team wouldn’t have fresh towels regularly in their shower room, there wouldn’t be bars of soap kept in good supply and woe of woes if the toilet paper ran out, JEEZ. And speaking of their shower room it’s us who keeps the floor immaculate so that the team members don’t have to wear shower shoes when washing the stink of the game off them. No athlete's foot for these athletes that's for sure. It was us who stacked up the team's dirty laundry that they would leave behind after a game, we had it sent out to the laundry service and made sure it was distributed properly when it was returned. Never had a team member bitched about losing a lucky hat, a jockstrap, a pair of under shorts, or what have you. Yeah, it was us who helped to keep the team looking good… and for the most part they treated us pretty well. But one of the players, the one people called "the greatest baseball player in the world" didn't treat us all that well when it came time for bonuses. You know the special holidays when you give your mailman, your doorman, your gym trainer a little bonus. The guy who empties your wastebasket if you're an office worker, the driver of your office car if you're a high and mighty executive, you know the ones who get that little extra at times like Christmas, New years, fuck, even Thanksgiving some folks are good enough to give you a bonus if you're deserving of it. Most of the team members always gave us hefty bonuses around the special times of year, but it was the one they called the greatest that shafted us all the time… He seemed to think he had it coming it to him the way we waited on him hand and foot. He had the attitude that his shit didn't stink. (And oh fuck man; believe you me, as pretty as he is his shit stinks. When he sits in his favorite stall farting and retching and shitting it stinks like no one's business.) And man, we were tired of it let me tell you. We always wondered how, if ever, we would be able to pay the guy back, give him his due so to speak…and on the day that I'm telling you about now fate stepped in and dealt us a lucky hand buds…

"And I knew that when he reached home plate after rounding the bases that a few of the team members would carry him off the field on their shoulders, the sort of ride a king deserves I like to call that," Dave commented, him also looking down at the bench we were standing around and like Chris he leered meanly and sadistically.

Chris smiled evilly and said, "Yeah, did you see the way they gripped him by his high socked calves? Fuck me hard guys, those fucking guys used his calves like they were handles while they were carrying him around the field and then into the locker room, right into *this* locker room. I'm telling you, I don't care how straight those mulligans are they couldn't wait to grab him by his high socks…"

"From the smell of it in here the champagne really flowed," I said, taking a hearty sniff of the musty and man scented air around us.

"Yeah, they probably wasted more than a hundred bottles of the cheap bubbly dousing each other with it," Chris said, stepping to the end of the bench and looking downward as if he were in love. "And I would bet that the world's greatest baseball player really got the worst of the dousing."

As Chris stood at the end of the bench and Dave and I stood at the sides of it, we all looked down now, *down*, at the prone, stretched out form lying on that bench. Actually, the prone, stretched out form lying on that bench was tied to it real tight with mounds of white cotton rope and the poor guy was gagged with a soggy navy blue dress sock that we had found lying on the floor. I guessed that the sock was his, seeing as he had come to the stadium all dressed, spruced and spiffy in a navy blue suit. The fucking guy always looked his best, on and off the field to be exact. We guessed that when he had changed up he didn't realize that one of his fancy silky socks had fallen to the floor before he locked his locker. It was right in front of his locker that we had found the sock and it was Chris who had decided to save it as a souvenir, until we found what we found that is, or was, however you prefer to say that. The navy blue nylon OTC sock was stretched tight around the lying down form's big bull sized neck and wedged between his teeth. Every time the guy chewed or tried to talk through his sock/gag he was treated to a mouth and throat-full of his own dress sock stink.

Chris hunkered down at the end of the bench where the lying down form's tied up navy blue thick high socked feet, minus his cleats were, his socked toes wiggling nervously under said high socks…

"Oh man, the greatest baseball player in the world's socks stink of leather cleat crap, feet smell and champagne, what an aroma," Chris swooned and we all laughed. "Fucking awesome game it was…"

The greatest baseball player in the world looked up at us in a mixture of horror and anger, he gritted his teeth over his sock/gag and reeled "Remme rho ruh rastards…" trying actually to say, "Let me go you bastards…" We all laughed meanly as he struggled in the tight bondage, grunting and groaning in a manly way behind the silk sock/ gag…and we knew that no one, *no one* would be coming to the locker room any time soon, seeing as it was our time to be in there and cleaning up now…

And when we had come to the locker room to do our cleaning jobs was when we found the world's greatest baseball player all tied up, tied down, (however you prefer to look at it) ,minus his baseball uniform shirt, minus his cleats, wearing just his baseball uniform pants tucked into his thick navy blue high socks…

"Man oh man you guys, whoever thought that *we* would have found the world's greatest baseball player, the world's most famous baseball player at the moment, all tied up in the most famous locker rooms in the world?" I asked my buddies Chris and Dave, watching as Chris hunkered down at the handsome baseball player's navy blue high socked feet.

Chris wrapped his palms around the baseball player's tied feet and pressed his nose and lips against the bottoms of them, inhaling the funky scent of sweat and man grime of a game played for three and a half hours in the hot sun and humidity. I watched as Chris reverently inhaled the scent of the world's greatest baseball player's socked toes as the guy wiggled them again in his socks. Chris really took in the odor of the guy's leathery cleats that he had been wearing earlier as it mixed with his male foot sweat and the champagne as it baked into his socks. I guessed that his cleats had been ceremoniously removed from his feet as he had been carried into and then around the locker room and then he was sprayed with champagne from all sides. Actually, the baseball player's cleats were on the floor right under the bench he was so well tethered to. Looking up at me with desperation showing in his almond shaped brown eyes the world's greatest baseball player sputtered, "Rhu, rhu ruys, rhu ran't rhu rhis rhu nee…" actually trying to say, "You guys can't do this to me." He followed up with, "Rook rhat ror rud rair, rhe's shniffing rhy roddamed shocks, ruff rall rhings," trying to say, "Look at your bud there, he's sniffing my goddamned socks all things!" I laughed as I looked down at him and said, "Yeah, what a way to take liberties with you huh bud?"

"Yeah, and knowing Chris, the foot and sock freak that he is that's not all he's going to be doing with your socks and feet oh great one," Dave snickered and he hunkered down at the baseball player's exposed chest area. "Oh man, do we have plans for you, you handsome fuck, we'll teach you to shaft us…"

Dave tweaked one of the baseball player's jutted up nipples and the poor tied guy blurted, "Rhat rhin rhe hell rhu ruys? Rhush rhut roes rhat ruy ran on rhuing rish ny roddamned shocks an rheet?" trying to blurt "What in the hell you guys? Just what does that guy plan on doing with my goddamned socks and feet?" It was too funny the way the guy tried so hard to talk through the foul smelling gag he was chewing on. When we had found him he wasn't gagged, but it was Chris who spied the sock lying on the floor right by his locker and decided to silence him a bit with it.

"Is this soggy dress sock yours great one?" Chris asked the tied down guy teasingly as he dangled the gold toe section of the navy blue sock over the baseball player's nose and mouth.

"Never mind that, GAWD, that stinks," the baseball player complained. "Just untie me so I can be on my way and you mugs can do your cleaning job in here!"

"Mugs are we?" Chris asked him, sounding seductive as he hunkered down next to his face, pulling the sock over the baseball player's trembling lips. "And as for untying your sexy ass, well, I can honestly say that that's going to be a long time in coming..." The look on the great baseball player's face as the sock was wedged between his teeth was classic, a real, "Oh God, gagging a guy with his smelly sock is a shitty thing to do to him" kind of look. But Chris had looked adoringly at the guy as he fed him the sock and then tied it tight behind his bull sized neck. I thought for sure that the baseball player would fly off the bench, had he not been tied to it when Chris pecked him on the cheek after gagging him. He really made a "RRRMMMFFF" sound that time... No doubt he was also having horrific thoughts at the comment Chris had made about not untying him any time soon...

"Yeah, and aren't you glad you switched to the style of high socks for this season oh great one?" I asked the baseball player as I too hunkered down at his chest area, opposite Dave.

I too gave one of his jutted up nips a good tweak and twist...

HAR, HAR, HAR, the baseball player was stretched tighter than a drum on his back on that bench in the locker room buds, easy pickings for us, tied down fucking tight, as I said, his smelly socked feet minus his cleats. His feet were tied good and secure to the bench and a length of rope extended down to the leg of the bench, keeping the homerun hitting slugger in place. Rope was twined snugly and tightly about his stomach region, over his thighs and looped around his knees as well, keeping him well balanced on the thin wooden bench. His muscular arms were pulled up over his head and tied off at the wrists with mounds of rope, the slack of the rope tethered to the leg under the bench he was on, much the same way his darling well-scented socked feet were. The bowling ball sized muscles in his biceps bulged involuntarily as he struggled to no avail to get untied. And to add to the sexiness of the bondage he was tied in he was still wearing his baseball uniform pants, them fitting him nice and tight and sexy in all the right places, and the bottoms of them tucked into those high socks of his that had Chris so enraptured. For any guy who wears a uniform for what he does for a living, to be tied up in that uniform is the sexiest and also most humiliating thing that could possibly happen to him. I surmised that he had taken his uniform shirt off himself after he had been carried into the locker room, but it was nowhere to be seen at the moment.

The tied down baseball player struggled mightily to use his teeth to get the sock/gag over them and was able to say, “You fucker, like I said in that interview I granted to that sleazy magazine reporter, I switched to the high socks style for luck! All baseball players know that their socks bring them luck, and sure as all fuck it did bring me luck today!” As he sputtered and ranted, that dress sock tied over his teeth now he tried his damndest to get loose, struggling real sexily to no reward.

“FUCKERS, untie me! I’ve had a hell of a season so far. Can’t believe that reporter asked me about my socks of all things, and now this, FUCK! And just for the record here, what did you mean when you said you all had plans for me? I never shafted you mugs, you guys have a job to do and that’s that!”

Chris looked up at the greatest baseball player in the world where he was hunkered down at his navy blue high socked feet and squeezed and caressed them at the arches, inching his pinkies over the tied up guy’s inlets.

“What do you think we plan on doing with you oh great one?” Chris teased the tied up tied down baseball player and then in a fast motion scribbled his fingertips all over the bottoms of his socked feet.

“YAHHHHHHHHHHH!!!! H-hey, that tickles Mister!” the great slugger prattled loudly. “What’s the big idea??? Don’t be taking liberties with me like this! FUCKER!!!”

“Good thing you worked that sock out of your mouth huh buddy?” Chris razzed the guy. “If you were to laugh your head off while gagged and being tickled you could choke real badly…” As the baseball player struggled and squirmed in his bondage and as Chris tickled the bottoms of his socked feet I and Dave busied ourselves again tweaking and twisting his nipples a few times each.

"H-hey, HA, HA, HA, HA, HA, HA, holy fucking fucks, what in the hell goes on here?" the baseball player bantered as his nearly smooth muscular chest heaved up and down as we twisted the fuck out of his nubs. "Those are my goddamned tits you're makin' sport with there Sports!"

He had an olive complexioned robust and rock hard chest, huge muscular pecs that bounced involuntarily as he struggled and his tits that we were playing with were the size of silver dollars. They were as pointy as two new pencil erasers... Dave and I each squeezed and twisted one of the greatest baseball player's nebulous nubs as he laughed crazily as Chris continued tickling his socked feet.

"HAHAHAHAHAHA, what a twisted turn of events this is!" the baseball player prattled angrily. "And all because of a fucking joke..."

"Yeah, and how did you wind up in this position oh great one?" Chris asked the guy after he had stopped tickling his huge sweaty socked feet. "I figured it had to be some kind of joke that someone played on you... Was it the guys from the team you guys beat the tar out of out there on the field today? You have to figure how us finding you all tied up like this when we came in here really got our juices flowing oh great one..."

Lifting his head up between his tied up muscular arms the baseball player watched as Dave and I let go of his big tits. Behind the sock still tied just over his chin he breathed a loud sigh, almost as if he wished we hadn't let go and stopped tweaking and squeezing his two G-spots it seemed...

"I'm not telling you guys anything, what happens in a team's locker room is private and...WHOOOOOOO, HAHAHAHAHA!!!!" the baseball player began but Chris cut his banter short by starting to tickle his prized feet again. "OH GAWD, stop, stop it man!"

His tied up feet wriggled and wiggled sexily as Chris pressed his fingertips against the bottoms of them, gliding his hands up and down and up and down. The moist cotton of his socks felt wonderful to Chris as he did his thing.

"Tell us how you wound up tied up tied down buddy," Dave snickered as he took the sock/gag off the baseball player's chin and followed up by giving one of the guy's nipples a good squeeze and twist.

While Dave did that I strummed my fingers over the baseball player's ribs, tickling him there as well.

"OKAY, okay, just stop tickling me and squeezing my goddamned tits huh???" the handsome baseball player ranted through clenched teeth, looking up at Dave as he held the soggy dress sock up. "And if it'll keep you from gagging me with that damned sock I'll tell you what you want to know!"

Just to torment him a tad more we continued tickling him and twisting his nipples like they were bottle caps. As I figured would happen he started to make a tent in his baseball uniform pants…

"OOOOOOOO FUCK, OH SHIT, HA, ha, ha, ha, ha, ha, ha, ha, ha, ha, ha, ha, ha, ha, ha!!!" the great baseball player laughed and cackled.

Chris smiled fiendishly up at us as we took turns squeezing the baseball player's tits, twisting them, kneading them and tickling his ribs area. Dave and I watched then as Chris slurped the sweaty juice from the baseball player's socked toes. Chris held the ace baseball player's socked feet tight in the palms of his hands and sucked his randy toes.

"Fucking guy man, ha, ha, ha, ha, ha, ha, ha, ha, ha, ha, ha!!!!" the greatest baseball player in the world guffawed as Dave and I both tickled his ribs now, his nipples jutted up and real hard from the way we had treated them. "First he gags me with my soggy dress sock, then he tickles my damned feet, and now he's sucking my goddamned stinky toes through my socks…HAR, HAR, HAR, HAR, HAR, HAR!!!!!"

"Yeah, that's about the long and short of it oh great one," I teased the poor tied up tied down guy.

After tickling him and sucking his socked toes and tweaking his nipples for a good half hour we finally stopped. The baseball player was breathless as I held his head up by the back of his neck and let him sip down some mineral water from a bottle of Poland Spring…

"TH-thanks man, I needed a good drink," the baseball player grunted and cleared his throat.

Moments later Dave and I were sitting on the floor at the sides of the bench that the great baseball player was tied to… Chris of course was hunkered down in front of the guy's tied feet, inhaling their funky odor.

"So tell us oh great one, how did a big strong boy like you wind up tied up tied down to that bench you're on?" I asked the baseball player and reached up to squeeze one of his hard and erect nipples.

"Fuckers, like I said if it'll save me being tickled and tit tortured and sock gagged by you perverts I'll tell you," he seethed through clenched teeth.

"Well, I wouldn't say it'll save you from being tickled and tormented, but it might take some time off your upcoming next round of being tickled," Chris said and squeezed the baseball player's moist socked toes.

He wriggled them in Chris' grasp and to Chris it felt great let me tell you…

"Fuckers, hell of a way to take liberties with a baseball player of my stature and high standing," the baseball player complained.

"And of your high socks," Chris laughed and ran a hand up the great one's high socked calves.

"Yeah, that too, my goddamned high socks that you seem to be in love with," the baseball player said with his head lifted up as he looked across at himself and down at Chris in anger. "Like I said, a baseball player knows that his socks bring him luck, and I know that by showing off my socks it brings me even more luck..."

"But not today huh bud?" Chris asked reveling in the sight of the baseball player's socked feet right in his face. "Today these high socks of yours seem to have brought you some bad fucking luck, HAR, HAR, HAR for you."

Dave pressed a hand against the baseball player's forehead and gently pushed his head back down on the bench.

"Spill it bud, how'd you wind up tied up like you are?" Dave asked. "And you can look at us not untying you as payback for the shitty way you've treated us..."

The baseball player licked his lips and began...

"It was all because of a joke a few of my teammates decided to play on me," the baseball player said. "It wasn't guys from the opposing team that we bested today. It was part of the reason they carried me off the field. They had planned this from the get-go..."

"Which ones of your teammates did this to you?" Chris asked and kissed the bottoms of the great baseball player's feet.

As Chris kissed his socked feet the baseball player took a deep breath, squirmed miserably in the tight bondage and the tent in his uniform pants trickled a good dollop of pre cum. A look of disbelief came over the guy's prettily handsome face as Chris again kissed his awesome feet.

"It was Johnny, George and Derek," the baseball player replied.

Chris looked up at him over his tied down muscular bulk and

said, “Hmmm, Johnny and George carried you off the field after you hit that homerun and won the game for them.”

“Yeah, that was fucking awesome,” the greatest baseball player in the world swooned and closed his eyes in ecstasy for a moment, obviously reliving the moment in his mind as he hit the homerun that made history.

He had trotted around the bases and then wound up perched on his two teammate’s shoulders when he’d reached home plate. I recalled how Johnny and George had run over to him, squatted down and grabbed his legs, hoisting him quickly to their shoulders like a king of sorts. I thought about how they had held him there facing the crowd and how the fans cheered. As Johnny and George kept the greatest baseball player in the world balanced on their shoulders, holding tight to his socked calves the guy smiled his killer smile and waved at his adoring fans. Then they carried him across the field and into the team’s locker room. The crowd went even wilder.

“OHHHHHH, OH GAWD, you guys can’t do this to me!!” the greatest baseball player in the world was crooning in a mixture of anger and ecstasy a few moments later as we took even further liberties with him. He was now blindfolded with the long navy blue dress sock that we had gagged him with earlier and now he was writhing on the bench he was bound to. He was trying desperately at that point to get loose as Dave and I sucked one of his jutted up nipples each, really nursing on them. We slurped at his big nipples and Chris scoffed the sweaty sap from his socked toes, holding tight to the baseball player’s arches as he did so. As he was used in this fashion the tent in the baseball player’s uniform pants dribbled more beads of pre-seed, really staining his crotch area real sleazy and sexily…

“Fucking guys’ man, you can’t be doing this to me, what a way to take liberties!!” the baseball player prattled.

“Just think about the ecstasy you felt when George and Johnny carried you off the field," Chris said and quickly resumed slurping his socked toes while Dave and I ate his tits with gusto.

"Yeah, that was real cool, but they didn't suck my tits and smelly toes!!" the baseball player snarled angrily, his teeth clenched behind his blindfolded face.

"Nah, they just tied you the fuck up bud," Dave laughed and slurped the great baseball player's nipple quickly back into his mouth.

"UHHHHHHH!!!!" the baseball player heaved, his chest jutting upwards and we sucked his nipples more liberally.

Chris watched as Dave and I really sucked the leathery flesh of the great baseball player's tits, really stretching them up and working them. My cock was hard as a rock in my pants and I felt like I could cum without even touching myself there…

"Tell us why your teammates decided to tie you the fuck up bud," Chris said from the baseball player's socked feet, as he pressed his thumbs against the bottoms of them.

"After they carried me into the locker room they kept me perched up on their shoulders for the champagne festivities," the tied up blindfolded baseball player said breathlessly.

As he spoke we went on sucking the fuck out of his big tits, lapping at the tips of them, chewing on the meat of them. Chris continued his oral assault on the guy's stinking socked feet. As figured he explained how he had gotten the most and the worst of the champagne dousing. While George and Johnny carried him past his locker and while he was being sprayed with champagne up there was when someone did the honors of taking his cleats off his high socked feet. His feet were doused with champagne as he sat atop his teammate's shoulders. It was said that by baptizing his socked feet they were thanking those feet for being swift and mighty when they had propelled him around the bases. From up on his teammate's shoulders he said he felt honored and whooped it up along with them. He himself had taken his uniform shirt off and thrown it into the throng of his cheering buddies. He figured whoever caught that damned shirt had kept it.

"After all the cheering, after all the pats on the ass they gave me, after soaking me liberally with champagne and when they couldn't bear my weight on their shoulders anymore my buddies let me down," the great baseball player went on, just as breathlessly as we played suck with his sensitive nipples.

Chris was pecking delicate kisses on the baseball player's socked soaked toes…

"While some of our buddies stripped down and made their way to the showers George, Johnny and I hung out by my locker," the greatest baseball player in the world went on. "We were scoffing down some of the cheap bubbly and then Derek thought oh how fun it would be to tie me to the bench right next to my damned locker… We all hawed and laughed about how ridiculous that sounded until Derek produced the goddamned rope. It was said that it would bring the team luck in the next game… I tried to resist but it was three on one and in what seemed like no time they had me tied the way you see me now. All the other guys on the team thought I looked real funny tied up in just my high socks and baseball uniform pants…"

The baseball player stopped speaking momentarily to breathe heavily as we sucked his nipples and rubbed his chest and Chris lapped at the bottoms of his socked feet, holding him tight by the toes…

"When they were all dressed in street clothes and filing out I ranted and screamed for someone to fucking untie me," he continued. "But they left me here; saying that they had no doubt that the guys who clean the locker room would be along shortly to untie me…"

At that we all laughed meanly…

"I suppose they didn't figure on you guys not untying me, GAWD, if they could see me now," the baseball player seethed. "GAWD, if I could see now it would be great…"

"HAR, har, har for you again bud," Chris laughed. "So now that we know how you wound up like this lets get back to some real fun here…"

"OH NO, NO, please don't…" the great baseball player pleaded as Chris began again scribbling his fingertips all over the bottoms of his socked feet.

By then the baseball player's high socks were soaked not only with his feet sweat but with Chris' saliva as well. The way we had worked his nipples Chris had really worked the guy's socked feet. Once the guy was worked up enough in the crotch we had resumed tickling him, and we had decided he would stay blindfolded for that. When a guy is blindfolded while being tickled the sensations are heightened hundreds of percent…

So, as Chris tickled the great baseball player's feet Dave and I sucked his nipples and tickled his ribs…and even his armpits…

That really got the poor guy sweating, swearing and laughing…

About an hour later we were still tickling the greatest baseball player in the world…

At that point his cock was really leaking pre cum in his uniform pants. As we tickled him, sucked his nipples and sniffed his socks we suddenly heard a loud male voice call out, "What in all hell is going on here???"

We all looked up to see a nightshift security guard standing at the end of the row of lockers… As we all stood up I reached down to take the sock blindfold off the tied up tied down guy.

"Oh sweet balls, thank God help has arrived," the baseball player grunted. “Sam, these guys have been tormenting the fucking fuck out of me…”

The Security Guard looked at all of us, folded his arms and pursed his lips…

A short while later we were all stomping out of the locker room via the back way. The security guard had threatened to have us thrown in jail for what we had done to the poor baseball player. As we stomped out of there the baseball player’s high socks were sticking out of Chris’ back pocket of his pants. I had the guy’s dress sock that we had used to gag and blindfold him with. Dave said just knowing what we had done was memory enough for him. As the door of the locker room closed behind us the sounds of the greatest baseball player laughing his head off was still being heard. You see, the nightshift security guard said he would let us off with a warning if we didn’t tell anyone about his fetish for bare baseball player feet… As we exited the locker room Sam the security guard was now making sport of lick tickling the greatest baseball player in the world’s bare and smelly feet…

Prime Muscle's Green Speedo

Ten PM, GAWD, my buddy Al realized he had just about overstayed his time at the gym that night. He was so involved in pumping iron, hoisting those weights, sweating it out that he hadn't noticed the time. As he showered off and prepared to make his way to the Jacuzzi for twenty relaxing muscle soothing minutes he thought about how he really needed to join one of those twenty four hour gyms. The gym that Al works out at on a regular basis closes promptly every night at eleven, not convenient for a guy like my buddy Al who works out with gusto on a regular goddamn basis. Members are expected to start winding down their workouts, their swim laps and their Jacuzzi and steam room and sauna time around ten fifteen so that they can be out punctually by eleven. Al had been a member in good standing for the last two and a half years at the gym so he didn't think that the closing staff would mind if he overstayed his welcome by ten or fifteen minutes. Man oh fucking man, as my good muscle bound buddy stepped out of that shower and pulled on his light green colored Speedo boxer shorts style swim trunks he had no idea just how late the closing staff of the gym would have him there that night. Wearing just his green Speedo swim trunks buttoned up at the sides and a towel draped around his big bull neck Al made his way to the Jacuzzi and swimming pool area of the gym, all two hundred muscular pounds of him. Fuck, my buddy Al is prime muscle man, totally grade A choice beef… Al has dark short cut hair, sinister looking deep brown eyes and at the tender age of thirty-three the body of a god. At nearly six feet tall he has shoulders as wide as a doorway, curled and overly muscular biceps and huge triceps, a massive chest adorned with two of the fleshiest and meatiest nipples you've ever seen, stomach muscles like knotted thick cable and legs built as strong as tree trunks… Al works out six days a week for at least four hours, been doing that ever since we were teenagers. You can imagine that there is no shortage of ladies in my buddies' life. And after the particular night at the gym that I am relating herein there would be no shortage of guys in his life either…

As I said Al emerged from the shower area in his nylon button-up at the sides green Speedo boxer trunks. He had a towel draped around his massive neck and he headed for the Jacuzzi and pool area in the underground section of the gym. His long and thick beefy tool was semi hard in his Speedo. Fuck, after a hard workout most guys are exhausted and can't even think about laying a good sized boner. Not my buddy Al, he's a virtual twenty-four hour a day hard on. With his head held high and his cock now more than slightly chubbed up in his Speedo Al hung his towel on a hook and stepped over to the Jacuzzi. Al saw that there was one other body builder in the Jacuzzi, a blond hunky Adonis type that he'd seen numerous times at the gym while he was working out.

"Hey there bud," Al said to the guy in a gruff sounding tone of voice as he stepped slowly into the steaming and cascading jet stream water.

"Hey, how're you doin' there?" the blond Adonis responded as Al sat down next to him on the underwater ledge, right next to the jet stream by his lower back.

"Ahhhhhhh, *now* I feel great," Al said and laid his head slightly back.

The two muscle gods sat there side by side, their massive chests just above the water level, their nipples jutting out and torched up from the heat of the Jacuzzi.

"Good workout?" the blond guy asked Al and squeezed one of his thighs.

"*Hard* workout is more like it man," Al said. "Fuck, but I really worked myself over tonight."

"Yeah, I saw you really pumping iron bud," the Adonis said, holding up an open hand. "I'm Steve."

"Al, good to meet you Steve," Al said and really pumped the blond guy's hand. "Yeah, hard fucking workout, but it's the only way to stay in shape."

"Amen to that," Steve said and let go of Al's hand, letting it settle back under the water. "I see you here nearly all the time."

"That's me bud, a real gym rat," Al laughed and felt Steve's hand give his thigh another squeeze. "Although after tonight I wonder if the staff of this place will let me back in here."

"What do you mean?" Steve asked.

"Well, it's getting close to closing time and we're still in this Jacuzzi," Al said. "They really don't like it when members overstay their time. They like to close up on schedule."

"Well, they'll just have to give us the extra time huh?" Steve asked in reply. "I mean, we pay our membership dues every month, so fuck them."

"Yeah, putting it that way I can see what you mean," Al said and leaned his head back, looking up at the ceiling. "Ahhh man, but this sure does feel great after a hard and grueling workout…"

"You know, I sometimes work as a personal trainer here at the gym," Steve said to Al. "Maybe some time we can hook up and I'll really put you through some paces, work you over real good. What do you say Al?"

"Hell, maybe I'll take you up on that offer some time Steve," Al replied.

"Good deal then," Steve said and again held up his open hand.

Al shook Steve's hand and then the two men enjoyed the heat of the cascading water in the Jacuzzi.

"Yeah, you look like you would be able to really withstand one of my workout routines Al," Steve said dreamily and gave Al's thigh yet another squeeze under the water. "I'll work you out real hard buddy…"

Just then, another muscle guy walked into the Jacuzzi area clad in a pair of navy blue boxer style swim trunks. He and Steve looked at each other, grinned conspiratorially and he hung up his towel. The five feet ten inch tall muscle guy with dark wavy hair and brown eyes made his way into the Jacuzzi.

"Hey there, looks like we got more company Al," Steve said, again giving Al's thigh a tight squeeze under the water, this time perilously close to his crotch.

"Huh?" Al said leaning his head forward and glancing questioningly at Steve after having had the guy just feel him up a third time under the water.

"Hey there guys," the brown haired guy said in greeting, settling down next to Al. "Ahhhhh, feels awesome in here."

"Hi there, I'm Steve and this muscle boy is Al," Steve said, reaching across Al's torso with his hand open. "Looks like all three of us are goin' to be getting a reprimand for overstaying closing time here at the gym tonight."

"I'm Eddie," the brown haired guy said and took Steve's hand.

The two men shook hands, accidentally (?) rubbing their wrists against Al's chest, or more precisely his torched up and fleshy nipples…

"Whoooa!!" Al suddenly grunted with a grin on his handsome face and nearly bolted out of the Jacuzzi.

"Sorry Al didn't mean to do that," Steve said as Eddie shook Al's hand, a look of bewilderment on Al's face.

"N-no harm done I suppose," Al said as Eddie let go of his hand. "Just that for a guy I have real sensitive man tits, know what I mean?"

"I know what you mean buddy," Eddie said, glancing down at his own torched up nipples in the heat of the steaming Jacuzzi. "Not many guys will admit to that, *but I do*. Fuck, every time my girlfriend even tweaks my damned nubs she knows she can get her way every goddamned time."

"Hmmm, I guess mine are too," Steve said, grinning as he took his nipples in his fingers and thumbs and squeezed and twisted them. "OHHHH man that does feel great! Although I don't have a girlfriend at this time to work 'em over for me."

At that the three muscle bound men laughed heartily and ruggedly…

"Can't believe we're sittin' here cookin' in a Jacuzzi and talking about our man tits," Al guffawed.

"What happens exactly when your man tits are worked on Al?" Steve asked and turned to face Al in the Jacuzzi, brazenly giving one his fleshy nipples a hard squeeze.

"H-hey bud, easy there, no sampling the merchandise or takin' liberties, know what I mean?" Al grunted, still trying to maintain a smile when from his other side Eddie gave his other nipple a hard tweak followed by a twist. "Ohhhhh fuck, looks like I got two tit freaks here tonight."

"So what exactly happens bud?" Steve asked Al a second time.

"It, it gets me all boned and horned up man," Al said breathlessly from the heat of the Jacuzzi and having had both his nipples tweaked. "Fuck, every time my girl squeezes my man tits it gives me a major-sized boner. She calls 'em the control knobs for my cock." Then, suddenly, to Al's utter shock and total amazement he felt Steve's palm moving over the bulge in his Speedo under the cascading and steaming water...

"Shit, that's no lie," Steve said. "Feels like you're the man of steel down here Al."

"H-hey man, wh-what the fuck do you pervs think you're doin' here?" Al grunted and turned his head abruptly as Eddie gave his nipple yet another hard tweak and twist as Steve rubbed his palm hard against his hardness in his Speedo. "Shit bud, told you no sampling the merchandise or takin' liberties here and.... Ohhhhrrrrr fuck, n-now you two pervs have really done it!!!"

Al pressed his elbows hard against the outside ledge of the Jacuzzi and in a quick move bolted out of the swirling water. He balanced himself on wobbly feet at the edge of the Jacuzzi, looking down at the throbbing chub in his tight green Speedo and his torched up and tweaked nipples.

"Ohhhhhhrrr f-fuck, th-this is mortifying but I can't help it you bastards," Al grunted, looking down at the two men in the Jacuzzi as they looked up at him, watching the beginnings of cum stains form on the front of Al's water soaked Speedo. "G-goin' to shoot my damned load of power spunk like gangbusters here you guys!!"

"Shit, let us apologize by helping you out there bud," Steve said with a grin and along with Eddie climbed out of the Jacuzzi.

Standing there shuddering Al placed a hand over his crotch and goose bumps broke out all over his well-muscled body…

"Arrrrrrhhh shiittt, got to hold it back you mugs, this is embarrassin' shit here!!" Al grunted throatily.

Steve and Eddie stood at Al's sides, grabbed his arms and yanked them roughly behind him…

"Wh-*what are you mugs doin'*?" Al blurted, looking down at his throbbing chubbed up cock in his Speedo. *"Holy fucking shit you bastards!!!"*

Eddie held Al's arms behind him at the wrists as Steve stroked the hard on in his green Speedo.

"Ohhhhhhrrr GAWD, no, no you mugs, I was tryin' to hold it back and now…ohhhhrrrr fuck," Al groaned in the forced ecstasy.

The muscleman arched his well-toned body forward and as he tried to pull out of Eddie's strong grasp Steve quickly grabbed the guy as well. Standing there balanced against the edge of the Jacuzzi with the two men holding his muscular arms behind him Al shot a hefty sized load of ball juice.

"F-fuckers, perverts," Al grunted, squirming back and forth as his ball juice filled his Speedo. "Jacked me off in my damned Speedo!! Ohhhhh yeah, fucking A you pervs!!!"

"Fuck man, look at him cum, his girlfriend sure knows what the hell she's doing," Steve said jovially as he and Eddie held tight to their captured prey. "His man tits really are the control knobs for his cock."

"Arrrhhhhh f-fuck, perverts, *fuckers*," Al seethed in a mixture of ecstasy and anger at the same time as he seemed to shoot his load more and more uncontrollably. "Never had no guys get me off before!! Shit!!"

When he was done Steve and Eddie let go of him and my muscle buddy stood there between the two men catching his breath, bathed in the steamy water of the Jacuzzi and his own sweat, the scent of his cum wafting up at them from his Speedo.

"F-fuck, *now look at this shit*," Al complained bitterly, just as two of the gym's instructors walked into the pool and Jacuzzi area. "Shit, now I'm all slimy and messy in my damned Speedo. I should pulverize you jokesters for this!"

With looks of guilt etched on their faces the three musclemen looked up at the two gym instructors, both of them clad in the gym's uniform of a red tee shirt with the gym's logo on the back of it and black shorts as they approached them. Steve and Eddie each grabbed one of Al's upper arms…

"Shit, let go of me you mugs," Al seethed in a whispering sound of voice. "I ain't vouching for the two of you here. Bet they'll revoke all of our memberships for this shit! GAWD, of all things, to jack a dude off in his Speedo…"

"Hey guys, it's near closing time," Lawrence, a short haired, dark eyed muscular guy of African American descent said to the three musclemen as they stood over the Jacuzzi. "Time to wrap it up and start heading on out."

"Say, what's going on here?" Todd, a five foot seven lanky and well-toned guy with short brown hair and friendly looking eyes asked no one in general.

Todd's eyes were trained on Al, who stood there with Steve and Eddie holding his arms out at his sides, the cum stains evident on his green and well packed Speedo.

"Uh, nothing bud," Steve said, trying to act as nonchalant as possible.

"Nothing huh?" Al barked, glancing down at the cum stain on his Speedo and then glancing at the two men at his sides as they tightened their grips on his arms, a scowl on his face. "These two clowns just jacked me the fuck off in my damned Speedo. Fuck, two pervs that they are played tweak and squeeze with my damned man tits and got me all worked up. *Shit,* now I got a real slimy load of my power spunk in my Speedo. I'm no faggot here buds!" "Is that so Sir?" Todd asked Al as he and Lawrence approached the three muscle brutes, still standing there water sopped and Al of course cum sopped.

"Yeah, it's so, these two fucking perverts should have their gym memberships revoked and be thrown the fuck out of here, *permanently*," Al grumbled glancing at the two men holding tight to his arms at his sides as the two gym instructors now stood before them. "Fuck, let go of me you two mugs, what are you guys, in love with me or somethin'?"

"Well, we would need some proof of what you're insinuating here Sir," Todd said with a wicked looking grin on his face.

"Proof? *You need proof?*" Al barked at the two instructors. "Tell me something guys, how many members here complain of what the hell I'm accusing these two jokesters of?"

Then, to Al's further astonishment and shock the two gym instructors undid the side buttons of his Speedo and pulled it down in the front, revealing the mess of cum in it and caked onto Al's pubic bush, his semi hard cock and his big hairy balls. Eddie and Steve held tighter to Al's arms as a look of more than disbelief came over my buddies' handsome face…

"Yeah, it sure looks like you've been jacked off Sir," Lawrence said, brazenly swirling a long fingertip into the soupy mess in Al's Speedo, poking his fingertip into Al's wide sexy slit.

"Huhhhhhhhh!!!!" Al grunted, suddenly breathless over this twisted turn of events and having his piss hole poked. "H-hey man, wh-what the fuck're you doin'?"

Then, Lawrence took a handful of Al's slimy and sensitive cock and hefted the big meat pole straight up, holding it tight, tugging at it, as Todd ran a finger along the bottom of Al's plum sized juicy balls.

"Yeah, he's got it all over himself," Todd said to Lawrence, holding up a cum slicked finger. "Looks like these two guys did jack him off."

"Wh-what are you pervs doin' here?" Al gasped as Lawrence held tighter to his now erect cock and Eddie and Steve held tighter to his muscular arms, pulling them behind him. "G-GAWD, I'm getting the distinct feeling I've been had somehow…"

"The least we can do for your trouble Sir is to help clean you up a bit," Todd said, again sliding a finger over Al's cum slicked balls and then slurping his finger into his mouth.

"Wh-what do you pervs got in mind here?" Al grunted, arching his upper muscular body forward.

The muscleman watched in utter amazement as the two gym instructors squatted down in front of him and began licking and slurping his cum out of and off his Speedo.

"Ohhhhhhrrrrr f-fuck," Al gasped as Lawrence slurped his cum slicked hard on deep into his craw and began working lip magic on it, sucking it for all he was worth. "GAWDS, you perverts, you *fuckers*, d-don't be suckin' my meat stick so soon after I've shot a load, *fuck*, I'm all sensitive and sexy down there right now..."

"I'll say you're sexy," Steve said snidely, holding tighter to Al's arm and gave one of his earlobes a suck.

"Hey, I wonder how many loads we can get from this big muscle guy," Todd said with a grin and ran his tongue over Al's balls, licking up the cum on them as he did so.

"Heh, keep workin' me the way you are and you'll find out pervert," Al seethed. "Ohhhhrrrr yeah, you keep this shit up and you're goin' to find out the hard way that I'm a twenty-four hour beat-off machine!"

"That explains the beefy hard on in your Speedo when you came into the Jacuzzi so soon after working out muscle head," Steve said, leaned down and slurped one of Al's nipples heartily into his mouth, still managing to hold Al's arm behind him at the same time.

"Hmmmm, now that seems appetizing," Eddie said with a grin from Al's other side, leaning down and slurping Al's other nipple into his mouth.

"Ahhhhhhhh f-fuckers, eatin' my big fat man tits," Al seethed, looking down, watching as his cock and balls were worked and now his nipples. "F-fuck, never had no guy suck my cock or eat my man tits before... Now lookit this shit, got me four pervs treating me like I was the main course at a buffet dinner!"

Lawrence and Todd switched places, Todd now sucking the muscleman's big throbbing cock while Lawrence went to town slurping and suckling his juicy balls. Up above Steve and Eddie held Al tightly in place by his upper arms and ate and ate his fleshy nipples with utter gusto...

“UHHHHHHH, getting close now you man eaters,” Al grunted. “Goin’ to shoot a second load for you fucking jokesters!!”

At that Todd and Lawrence quickly stopped working the muscleman’s cock and balls, pulled his green Speedo up in front and stroked him in it, taking turns as Steve and Eddie went on slurping and sucking his nipples.

“OHHHHHRRRRR f-fuck, GAWD,” Al seethed in ecstasy. “G-got me shootin’ my damned load in my Speedo again!!! Wh-what’s up with that shit anyway?”

“Just having you refill it for us with another treat of your ball juice,” Todd said laughingly, rubbing the palm of his hand over Al’s throbbing boner in his Speedo, forcing and working as much of the muscleman’s good stuff from it.

A few moments later with Steve and Eddie still holding Al’s arms tightly behind him the four men looked hungrily at Al’s cum soaked crotch while the muscleman caught his breath. His cock was semi hard and slimy in his Speedo, his nuts were throbbing from the tongue thrashing they’d been dealt and his nipples were sucked up like two ripe cherries on his massive chest…

“Huhhhhhhh, got my nut twice buds,” Al panted. “This turned out to be some fucking night I got to tell you. Now if you mugs will let go of me and let me dress we can all be on our way.”

But instead the two gym instructors took Al by his upper arms as Steve and Eddie let go of him. Todd and Lawrence forced Al’s arms back behind him as Steve and Eddie this time squatted at his cum soaked Speedo.

“GAWD, what now you jokesters?” Al grunted, still breathless.

“Okay you two, seeing as you guys started all this I guess it’s only right that you should sample his good stuff as well,” Lawrence said jovially.

Al watched in astonishment as Steve and Eddie pulled his Speedo back down in front again revealing the mess of ball juice that he had spurted into it.

"OHHHHHHRRR no, no, not again you pervs," Al grunted as Steve slowly slurped his semi hardness into his mouth, caressing it smoothly with his silky lips as he did so. "Ohhhhhrrrr shhhiiiiittt, bastards are fixing to get a third load of ball juice out of me, G-GAWD, I'm getting sore you fuckers!!"

"Well, you did say that you were a twenty-four hour beat off machine," Lawrence said with a grin as he and Todd held tighter to Al's arms. "Okay muscle head, up we go for this ride."

Al panted breathlessly as Lawrence and Todd lifted him a few inches off the floor all the while Steve sucked his again erect cock and Eddie lapped at his sweaty balls. Lawrence and Todd hoisted the muscleman slowly up and down, driving his cock in and out of Steve's eager mouth…

"OHHHHHRRR yeah, strong fuckers you guys are," Al seethed, watching as Steve chowed down heartily on his newly erect cock. "Liftin' me ain't no easy chore buds…"

The sounds of slurping, licking and sucking filled the humid air around the Jacuzzi and the pool as Al was sucked off for the third time that evening…

"Huuuuuuuhhhhhhh!!! C-can't believe I'm goin' to shoot a third load you mugs," Al announced a few minutes later as Steve and Eddie switched places, Eddie now sucking the muscleman's cock as Steve lapped at his balls. "And so soon at that too…"

"And up we go even higher," Lawrence said with a grin.

Lawrence and Todd then held Al aloft by one arm and one leg each, the muscleman facing downward in a prone position now as he was sucked like crazy from underneath…

"Arrrhhhhhh fuckers, wh-what a position you mugs got me in now," Al panted as he was rocked up and down, his Speedo clad tight butt making a real pretty picture as underneath him Eddie sucked his cock and Steve lapped at his mangy balls. "Ohhhhhrrrrr yeah, I-I'm cummin' now you pervs!!"

That said Eddie quickly took the muscleman's cock out of his mouth, pulled his Speedo up in the front and grabbed hold of the throbbing bulge now in it. Al watched with his head craned forward and downward as Eddie held tight to his bulge in his green Speedo and Lawrence and Todd held him aloft by his arms and legs. Al shot a hefty-sized (third) load of ball juice…right into his Speedo, again. The muscleman's creamy load again sopped and slimed up the front section of his sexy Speedo, Lawrence and Todd still rocking him up and down as Eddie held tight to his spurting bulge.

"OHHHHHHHYYYUUUHHH!!!! M-my fuckin' head is spinnin' buds," Al seethed as he spurted glob after glob of his mess in his Speedo. "G-GAWD, got me creamin' in my damned Speedo again!! God almighty, my cock is sorer than a hustler's is on a busy Friday night…"

A few moments later Al was on his feet as Steve and Eddie again held his arms behind him. The four men stood surrounding the muscleman, stealing sucks, licks, slurps and even kisses on his erect and sensitive nipples…

Al's Speedo was again chock filled with his cum in front and his cock was semi hard and slimy within it, a ready treat for his four cum hungry, so called buddies of the evening.

"Fuckers, perverts, I should fuck you mugs up for this," Al gasped. *"And leave my man tits alone you mugs!!"*

"Hmmm, fuck us up, or just fuck us muscle boy?" Steve asked Al snidely. "Think you got enough of your good stuff left for that?"

"Want to find out faggot?" Al spat in the Adonis-like body builder's face. "Let go of me and then we'll see just how anxious you are to be eating my man tits…"

The four men laughed meanly and then Al found himself again being lifted in a prone position as the four men proceeded to lug him toward the steam room…

"Huhhhhhhhh!!!" Al panted. "Put me down buds, where are you fuckers takin' me? Shit, this is startin' to feel like kidnappin' here!"

The four men lugged their prize into the steam room, the heat and mist enveloping them as they entered…

"Th-the damned steam room?" Al asked as the men stretched him out atop a cushioned table.

His Speedo was again pulled down in front and gasping and gripping the sides of the table Al watched with his head raised as the four men took turns slurping his cum from his Speedo and stealing sucks on his sore cock…

When the muscleman was *again* hard as a rock it was decided that Steve would get the first ride on his overly used and abused cock…

"Ohhhhhrrrrr man, your ass hole is tighter than a woman's pussy you faggot," Al seethed up at the blond body builder as he settled slowly onto his cock.

"Yeah, and I'll just bet that you're going to treat it like a pussy muscle head," Steve grunted breathlessly in the heat of the steam room.

"ARRRHHHHHHHH yeahhhh, got that right you bastard," Al

said, gripped the sides of the table even tighter and began thrusting his hips up and down, plowing Steve's hole like a field. "Goddamned fuckers, perverts, all this just so you could make me shoot a few loads in my Speedo. Well, now I'm going to be shooting my loads in all of you, one at a goddamned time!!"

Steve rocked up and down almost involuntarily on Al's rock hardness as the muscleman treated his hole most savagely…

"Come on you mugs, line up behind this faggot, I got enough of my man juice to feed all your pussy holes!!" Al seethed and the mist of the steam enveloped the four men even more so…

Lawrence and Todd sucked and slurped Al's nipples and Eddie hunkered down at the muscleman's big bare feet, licking them and sucking his toes…

"Harrrrr yeah, your buddies are treating me like a damned buffet here faggot," Al grunted up at Steve as the body builder seemed to be impaled on his cock. "G-GAWD, suckin' my man tits and lickin' my smelly feet only bones me up all the more buds!!"

All the while the four men took turns being fucked by the handsome muscleman his green Speedo remained pulled down around his muscular thighs…

It was nearly two AM when five exhausted looking musclemen exited the gym that night, three of them dressed in business attire and two of them dressed in the uniform of the gym. All the men shook hands and went their ways…

The next morning the cleaning man found a very sticky and very cum stained green Speedo in the steam room of the gym…

Marcello

"I did it, I did it, I landed the account for the firm," Marcello was thinking joyously, smiling from ear to ear as he exited the elevator in the lobby of the luxurious office building where he had just attended a very important meeting. "I can't wait to see the expression on old man Bradshaw's face when he finds out that his boy wonder, *me*, landed one of the biggest accounts yet for the advertising firm."

Wearing a one thousand dollar charcoal colored business suit by Armani, complete with a white button down shirt, a silk black and white striped tie and matching pocket square all by Hermes and a pair of five hundred dollar lace-up wingtips by Stacy Adams the handsome executive made his way out of the office building. It was nearly five PM and the sun was still shining, though with hints of the evening peeking through. It was a mild night weather-wise in New York City. Clutching his leather attaché case that contained the signed contracts in hand he strode around the building toward the underground parking garage where he'd parked the company car he had arrived in earlier that day. Marcello had never had a doubt that he would land the multi-million dollar account for the advertising firm he worked for. Actually it had been Vice President James Bradshaw who had been reluctant to send the exotically handsome Marcello to the computer company in hopes of landing an account with them to do their new ad campaign. Marcello had heard it rumored in the company that Bradshaw saw him as a guy who got by on his looks. Granted, Marcello knew that his looks did help his cause when it came to making big dollar sized sales pitches, but he also knew that one needed the brains to back that up. And Marcello had the brains, he had the knowledge and the savvy and he resented that Bradshaw thought of him only as a pretty boy…or did he? Well, today he would prove the older man wrong when he got back to the office and told him that he had landed the account. And not only had the nearly six foot tall, well-toned and muscular dark haired and almond shaped eye Marcello landed the account, but he had managed to convince the board of directors of the computer company to sign a three year contract, locking them in real tight… Bradshaw had been after a two year deal; wait till he found out that it had been upped to three years.

As Marcello strode around the block of the office building toward the underground parking garage he couldn't help but notice how some of the passerby (both women and men) looked lustfully at him. His smile was what could be defined as a killer smile; the man had movie star looks. He was no stranger to people he'd never met before checking him out and ogling him. One guy who passed by him glanced down at Marcello's feet and seemed to take a deep breath. The handsome executive knew that when it came to his male admirers it was his feet they coveted, which was why the guy always made sure to be wearing the best shoes and the sexiest of socks. Somehow Marcello sort of got the feeling that his looks were not entirely lost on Vice President Bradshaw and somehow he got the feeling that that was why he'd sent him on this business venture. Maybe the older man didn't just think of him as a pretty boy, maybe he really did have faith in him, just that he didn't want to show it. Maybe the old coot was afraid it would cause Marcello to get what's called a swelled head. Well, it was too late for that Marcello thought, seeing as the head between his legs had swelled when the directors of the meeting signed the contracts. During the business proceedings behind the closed door of the conference room where he'd negotiated the advertising contract with the heads of the computer company Marcello did notice how a few times one of the gentlemen present and two of the women really seemed to be drinking in the sight of him. He managed to keep his mind on the business at hand, but to be perfectly honest thoughts of humping the two lovely women and making the gentleman watch while he did so played erotic havoc with his thoughts. That was one of his ultimate fantasies, to have two women at the same time while a jealous guy sat tied to a chair and watched helplessly, unable to join in the pleasures that Marcello was enjoying. A smirk came across his face as he pictured himself binding the guy from the meeting to a chair while the two lovely ladies awaited him on the bed. The guy would have been stripped to his underpants while tied up and then made to try to get loose so he could participate in the fun. But Marcello knew that with the way he tied knots that would never happen. The ladies would be all his... As the debonair business suited gentleman made his way into the underground garage his lips widened again into a broad smile, chuckling to himself at how well he had pulled off this venture.

"Ah Marcello, you truly are headed for the big time," he said to himself, straightening his tie as he walked toward the clerk in the booth of the parking garage, his heel taps clicking on the pavement and echoing in the wide open space of the garage. "The commission alone on this deal will be astronomical..."

Marcello handed his receipt and a nice hefty sized cash tip to the booth clerk and said, "There you are my good man..."

The clerk looked at the receipt, thanked Marcello for the tip and drew up a total for the few hours that Marcello had parked his company car in the garage. He then handed Marcello the keys to the vehicle. Marcello paid the bill out of the company's petty cash, thanked the booth clerk and made his way through the twists and turns of the deserted underground garage to his company car. As he approached his car he saw that it was the only one left in the section where he'd parked. Made sense he figured, seeing as the business day was just about at an end at that point. But it was when he sauntered around to the driver's side of the car that he noticed something that unnerved him, the door of the car on the driver's side was standing wide open.

"What in the hell?" Marcello whispered as he stepped next to the open door, placing his attaché case down on the ground next to the car. "I'm sure I closed this door when I parked here earlier..."

Suddenly, as if out of nowhere a figure dressed in a black ninja style outfit of sorts made its way from around the other side of the car.

"Hey, who are...?" Marcello began as the figure seemed to move with the speed of lightening.

Before the handsome suited gentleman could react the figure reached down, grabbed his attaché case and flung it across the deserted parking area.

"HEY!!!!" Marcello shouted angrily. "There are important papers in there!!"

The attaché case landed with a thud far away from the car and flew open; Marcello's important papers, signed contracts and copies of everything were suddenly all over the concrete ground.

"OH HOLY SHIT!!" Marcello hollered and dashed toward the papers strewn all over the ground.

Suddenly, the suited executive was grabbed from behind by the collars of his suit jacket and white shirt and yanked back, him nearly flying out of his expensive wingtips.

"ACCCCHHHH!!!" Marcello bellowed, one of his feet kicking out as he looked longingly at his prized signed contracts while at the same time trying to keep his balance.

"I love you suit guys, you come complete with handles and leashes," the assailant chuckled as he gripped Marcello's collars tighter.

His assailant quickly reached around him and before Marcello knew what was happening the ninja dressed figure had him by the knot in his tie.

"ACCCHHHH!!!" Marcello reeled again, ready to do battle with this joker for ruining his perfect and very eventful day.

As the figure peered out from the eye slits of his ninja style outfit he held Marcello tight by his necktie knot, yanking him forward, using the necktie as a leash of sorts.

"This way you handsome fuck," the person said in a deep throaty sounding voice, pulling Marcello further toward the back of the dank underground garage. "And not a sound…"

"Fuck you, I'm not going anywhere with you man!" Marcello railed and as he raised a fist, ready to pummel his assailant he was suddenly looking at the tip of a long knife. "OH HOLY SHIT!!!" The man dressed as a ninja was just about as tall as Marcello, shy a few inches perhaps, but with that knife in hand he might as well have been a thousand feet tall. Marcello found himself suddenly sweating in his silk socks as he realized he was going to be more than likely a mugging victim…or worse…

The mugger let go of Marcello's tie and held the knife up in plain view.

"Move it, back that way, away from your car," the mugger said demandingly, waving the knife in Marcello's direction. "If you don't do as I say I'll make a mess of that pretty face of yours…"

"Okay, okay, I'll give you whatever you want man," Marcello ranted through clenched teeth. "But can I at least pick up my papers? Those are signed documents and…"

But before Marcello could finish his sentence the mugger again grabbed him by his silk tie. This time though he twisted the executive's tie around the collar of his shirt till the knot and slack of it was at the back of Marcello's neck.

"ACCHHHHHHH…" Marcello choked as the length of his tie was pulled from his shirt collar and pressed against his sexy Adam's apple.

He then found himself being dragged along, forced to walk backwards as the mugger used his expensive necktie definitely like a leash. The handsome executive raised his hands and tried to pry the length of the necktie away from his neck. As he plodded helplessly backward, walking stupidly, he looked helplessly at his papers all over the ground of the parking garage…

"UHHHHHHH!!!!" Marcello grunted a few moments later as his assailant rammed him up against a concrete wall in the back-most section of the underground parking lot.

The terrified executive stood with his back against the wall, his hands clenched into fists at his sides as he caught his breath. His assailant held the knife straight up as Marcello undid his tie, gasping for air.

"Wh-what do you want man?" Marcello asked as he straightened his tie against the sides of his suit jacket. "I got money, I got credit cards, what do you want?"

The man in the ninja outfit laughed fiendishly, grabbed Marcello's chin with one hand, gripped it tight and held the side of the sharp knife against the executive's puckered lips.

"*Oh God no, no, please…I'll give you anything you want, I'll do whatever you say…"* Marcello pleaded, feeling totally helpless in the clutches of his unknown assailant.

"Yes you will you handsome fuck, you will give me what I want, and you will do whatever I say," the man whispered harshly and Marcello, the knife still against his lips nodded miserably. "Kiss the side of the knife…"

With no choice in the matter Marcello did as he was told. He puckered his exquisite lips as tightly as possible and planted a kiss on the side of the knife.

"Good man," the ninja mugger said with satisfaction and then trailed the knife down against Marcello's suited torso.

Marcello pressed himself up against the wall and sweated like crazy, panted in fear and grunted from the throat as the man trailed the knife over him, caressing him with it, until he got to the executive's crotch and held the knife there.

"NO, NO, whatever you want…" Marcello pleaded and to his surprise the man slid his tie off him and dropped it on the ground.

"I want your pretty suit, your shoes…and your under shorts…" the man said and Marcello looked at him as if he hadn't heard correctly.

"Y-you want what???" Marcello panted as the man moved the knife away from his crotch now.

"You heard me, we can start at the bottom or the top, that's up to you, make an executive decision you pretty fuck," the mugger said and as he pressed the tip of the knife against the side of Marcello's neck the handsome executive pulled himself to his wing-tipped tip toes.

"Okay, okay, but if you take my clothes how will I get out of here?" Marcello asked, tears in his eyes as the tip of the knife was slid against his neck and then away.

"As you high-powered executives are so fond of saying, that's not my problem," the mugger chuckled and then pressed the tip of the knife against Marcello's ribs. "Start with taking off your shoes…"

Marcello lowered himself down from his tiptoes and squatted partway down to undo the laces of his wingtips. As he did so his fingers trembled. Disbelief set in as he could not believe he was being mugged for his expensive and fine clothing. Standing quickly back up he slid his size ten and a half feet out of his shoes. The concrete ground of the parking garage felt cold beneath his thin sheer black OTC socks.

"Okay, up to you what's next, suit jacket or pants?" the mugger asked, kicking Marcello's shoes away next to where his tie was on the ground.

With his hands shaking Marcello proceeded to shuck off his suit jacket. He handed it to the mugger who folded it neatly and placed it atop the shoes on the ground.

"Wh-why are you doing this to me?" Marcello asked as he began unbuttoning his crisp white dress shirt, the underarms section of it now stained with his fear sweat.

"You're a smart business type guy, you figure it out," the ninja dressed mugger replied as Marcello then pulled the tails of his now unbuttoned shirt out of his suit pants, baring his robust, smooth and well-toned muscular chest.

As Marcello slid the shirt down his arms and off himself the mugger's eyes lit up in the slit of his ninja mask.

"Jeez, lookit that," the mugger said breathlessly, staring hungrily at Marcello's glorious fear sweated chest, his washboard abs, his gloriously big pecs, his jutted up hard nipples that looked like two pink pencil erasers and his wide as a doorway shoulders. Marcello's arms were muscular as well, his biceps were beautifully curved and his triceps were curled and sexy… The mugger took note of that as well as the man he had captured bared his chest…

Leaning against the concrete wall Marcello tossed his shirt atop the growing stack of his clothing on the ground of the garage. It wasn't lost on the exotic looking executive that this mugger lusted for him. Could that be why this guy had chosen him??? It was obvious he had been chosen by this guy, he knew where Marcello's car was parked after all…

Holding the knife straight up and in Marcello's immediate view the mugger reached forward and with his thumb and first fingers of one hand tweaked and twisted one of the executive's nebulous nipples.

"OOOOOOHHHH…" Marcello swooned and gyrated his sexy body against the wall, his back feeling the cold of the concrete.

"Like that eh you handsome fuck?" the mugger asked and squeezed Marcello's nipple tighter in his fingers and thumb.

"Fuck, hate to admit it, but yes, for a guy I have real sensitive tits," Marcello panted and the mugger brazenly leaned forward and slurped on Marcello's other nipple while holding tight to the first one. "OOOOOOOO, taking liberties with me here Mister, that's what you're doing…"

Looking down as he was taken advantage of Marcello saw that the knife was now pointing downward in the mugger's hand. As the guy slurped on one of his nipples and squeezed and twisted the other one the nearly stripped executive thought how now was his chance. The guy's tongue was like a snake as it darted out of the mouth slit of his ninja mask and licked and lapped at Marcello's nipple. The executive's head was spinning though and he was feeling forced ecstasy as his nipples were treated like a nursing mother's. He managed to collect his thoughts and as he was feasted on at the nipples Marcello clenched his hands into fists once more, ready to get himself out of this awful predicament. Breathing heavily Marcello began raising his muscular arms a little at a time…but when his arms were to the halfway point the mugger stopped working his nipples and the poor executive found the knife pressed against one of his overworked nipples.

"HUUUHHHHHH!!!" Marcello grunted, fearing that the guy would slice his tit right off his muscular chest.

"You were about to try something foolish you handsome fuck?" the mugger asked his captive.

"N-NO, no, nothing like that, not at all," Marcello jibber jabbered.

"Get the suit pants off, NOW!" the mugger roared. "And your under shorts, I'm sure a handsome fancy exec like you must be sporting some real sexy under shorts huh?"

"If, if you say so Mister," Marcello said, unbuttoning his suit trousers and feeling the weight of his cash filled wallet in the back pocket. "M-may I keep my wallet?"

Smiling evilly beneath his ninja mask the mugger said, "Sure, but I'll be taking all the cash that's in it pretty boy."

"Okay, okay," Marcello sighed miserably as his pants fell down around his socked ankles and pooled there.

As he stood there with his pants down around his ankles Marcello raised a hand and covered his handsome face. The mugger took in the sight before him, the awesome sight, and the breathtaking splendid sight of a huge stalk as it pointed straight out and erect between Marcello's tree trunks like muscular legs. As Marcello stepped out of his suit pants he sheepishly said, "As you can see I rarely wear under shorts" and moved his hand away from his face. He stared straight ahead and said, "You can have my socks if you prefer…"

"Nah, you can keep your socks pretty boy," the mugger said. "But this…oh this…"

Marcello did not look down; he could not bear to; he continued staring straight ahead as the man took hold of his fear hard knob and twisted it around back and forth a few times. The executive's testicles hung down low in their sexy sac and Marcello again covered his handsome face with one hand. Hard as rock and throbbing as he was, he was mortified. The man's hand felt like silk as it caressed and teased his hard manhood.

"With a cock of such mammoth proportions and balls so succulent its no wonder you were free-balling in your suit you handsome fuck," the mugger said. "You need all the room you can get for this beefy member of yours..."

As he was rudely handled and being taken liberties with Marcello could not even wish his boner to go down. Was he somehow enjoying all this he wondered? Was there a secret part of him that had become aroused at being held and used in this manner? Was that possible?

When the man let go of his knob Marcello slowly took his hand away from his face...

Standing there now in just his OTC black sheer striped socks by Stacy Adams with garters clipped to them Marcello saw that the mugger was gone. My God, as quickly as the guy had appeared he had just as quickly disappeared. Marcello quickly looked down to where he had piled his clothes and saw that they were gone as well...

"Oh fuck me, fuck me, I am really screwed here," Marcello said out loud and without thinking grabbed his stiff hard erection in one hand. With his back still against the wall Marcello slid to the ground and sat on his naked sexy ass. He stroked his throbbing hard cock slowly; his balls cupped in his other hand.

"Fucker took me by surprise, mugged me for my clothes," Marcello huffed as he stroked himself faster. "GAWD, I'm naked in a public place... fucking guy, handled my knob and played suck and twist with my tits...FUCKER!"

Marcello's deep voice echoed through the garage…

Somehow the danger of being seen in such a manner spurred the handsome executive on as he gripped his cock tighter and massaged his balls as he felt his load building in them. His piss slit dripped with pre cum…

"Said he would leave me my wallet, fucker took that too…" Marcello mumbled and then he leaned back a bit more and shot a hefty sized load of executive ball juice all over his stomach and chest areas. "OHHHHHHH, ohhhhhhhhh fuck yes, what a wank!"

He raised his socked feet up and yanked a few last times on his semi hard knob, a few last ropes of thick creamy splooge erupted from Marcello's cock…

"OHHHHHHHH…" he grunted when he was done.

His cum caked up on his stomach and chest areas and the executive slowly stood up on his socked feet. He looked around the public parking garage and wondered how in all fucks he was going to make his way out of there naked as he was. He didn't even have the ignition key to his company car. The mugger had taken that when he'd confiscated Marcello's suit jacket, seeing as the keys were in his suit jacket pocket. With his hand over his cock Marcello began making his way slowly toward his company car, remembering the cell phone that he had left in the glove compartment. He prayed that the door to the car was still open… Along the way he found his important papers and attaché case still where the mugger had tossed them. Thank God for small miracles Marcello thought. The naked but for his socks executive hunkered down and quickly shucked all the papers and documents into the attaché case. He would worry later about putting them all back in the proper order…

When he turned the bend to where his company car was parked he was overjoyed to find that the door on the driver's side was still open. With one hand still covering his cock and holding his attaché case in his other hand he dashed over to the car and got in, slamming the door shut behind him… He tossed the attaché case in the back seat…

With his hand shaking he reached over to the glove compartment and popped it open. He smiled widely at the sight of the cell phone. He looked up the phone number for the booth clerk in the parking garage and pressed "Send" to call the guy…

A few moments later the booth clerk came striding up to the car, a stack of clothes in his arms.

"Thanks man," Marcello said as he rolled the window of the car down.

"Glad I could be of assistance there handsome guy," the booth clerk said, handing Marcello the suit of clothes through the open window of thc car.

As the booth clerk walked away Marcello again smiled from ear to ear and said, "Marcello, you are one hell of a so and so…"

He looked over his suit, tie and shoes, saw they hadn't suffered all that much in the struggle scene and got out of the car to get dressed and head back to his office for his meeting with Vice President James Bradshaw…

In the Soup

I'm writing this with the hope that someone will find it, take it seriously and send someone, anyone to rescue me. I've been here now for a little more than a year and this is the first time that Master has allowed me the luxury of writing, so I figure I better make good use of the time. Sitting here in the position I'm in however I am still reminded of my situation and my status. I'm a prisoner and a slave, all at the same time. Master allows me to wear very little; he likes me to always be at the ready for him, which is pretty often. Sitting here clad in just a pair of black socks and the padlocked chastity belt that Master keeps on me practically at all times my shackled hands are shaking as I put this to paper. I know when the mail is picked up in the afternoons so I have to make sure this is with it and I am praying that it gets into the right hands back in the United States. Seeing as I worked as a security chief for a well-known jewelry company I am sending this to the head of a well-known security company. I am only praying that the guy takes it seriously. The butt-plug that Master keeps wedged inside me when not using my hole torments me and also keeps me reminded of my status to him. The damned thing is fat and long and to add to the misery it is also a vibrator. Its battery powered, remote controlled. As soon as it starts buzzing meanly inside me I'm to stop what I'm doing and high tail it to Master's room. Believe me when I tell you that when that thing is buzzing in my hole I can high tail anywhere on the double. That thing gets me moving in double time that is for sure. My nine-inch meat stick is hard as a rock in the chastity belt that Master keeps on me at all times. I am not allowed to touch my meat stick unless it is to piss with. If I shoot my load, even by accident while Master is working me over there is hell to be paid. The fact that my melon shaped ass cheeks are striped red and welted attests to the punishments I have endured for my indiscretions. Master uses a leather paddle, a leather strap, a Cain, the wooden side of a hairbrush and at times my own belt to wallop my ass when he feels that I am in need of punishment. A thin wooden spoon is used to whap my balls from time to time as well. Master likes my meat stick to always to be hard. He claims it keeps me frustrated and on my toes and always ready to serve him. Unfortunately he is right. Actually he is always right. I know better than to disagree with Master. Sometimes to really torment me Master keeps me securely tied to a marble statue of an erect man in his bedroom, my hole impaled on the massive phallus of the thing. While I'm lashed to the thing Master takes the chastity belt off me and marvels in my frustration and agony as my meat stick twitches in hardness and oozes pre cum. Straight up and hard it reaches just above my belly button. He insists that I truly love the thing that I have become, a sexually frustrated slave. My balls constantly ache from the lack of relief they suffer from. My balls being always filled and bulging with my creamy man juices also keeps me insanely horny and keeps them hanging painfully low. Master loves the sight of me bent over with my big balls dangling provocatively between my legs. Sometimes Master makes me bend over in a doubled over position and ties my wrists to my ankles and simply marvels at the sight of my balls as they dangle between my thighs from behind. The slightest touch to my poor balls gets me screaming and crying in an agony that I can't describe to you. One time when I accidentally shot my load when Master had simply touched my meat stick while inspecting me he slid a catheter into my wide sexy dick slit and left it in there for the better part of two whole days, along with the chastity belt locked on me. Every time he fucked me and my meat stick rubbed against the inside of that thing was agony. The catheter in my slit felt like a thousand needles pinching me all at the same time. The pressure was immense and maddening to say the least. Master is tending to business while I write this. As if I were a child he wants me out of his way and kept occupied while he is busy with his moneymaking tasks. I am also made to exercise constantly. That is what I do most of the time while Master is tending to work. Since coming to belong to Master my body has become more than rock hard, more than muscular and more than well toned. Fuck, the workouts that Master has me put through by two of the men that work for him have made my body into a work of art. I'm six feet four inches tall. I have deep dark brown eyes, wavy black hair, a thick mustache and a sexy, sexy cleft in my chin. I didn't have the cleft when Master acquired me. He hired a surgeon to create it for him. When it was done and healed Master and I stood in front of a mirror and looked at my new chin cleft. Master says I am his most extraordinary and beautiful possession. Standing in front of that mirror with my hands shackled behind me Master gave my butt a squeeze and kissed my cheek gently. My meat stick pounded long and hard in its chastity belt prison. Money is the one thing that Master has more than what he knows to do with. It is the reason he was able to afford to have me scooped up and brought to him more than a year ago now. To put it more bluntly Master bought me, from that nerdy next door neighbor of mine no less. I never thought that Freddy could have been in the business he was in when he came to my door that night after work and captured me. The fucking guy was able to nab me right out of my own apartment, if you can believe that. Whenever I saw Freddy I simply thought of him as a pleasant but nerdy and dorky type of guy, the kind you simply say hello to in the hallway of your luxury apartment building and keep walking. I should never have let him in that night when he knocked on my door. But alas, if he didn't capture me that night I'm sure he would have snagged me at some point.... You see, unfortunately for me I fit the bill perfectly for what Freddy's most recent customer was looking for...

My name is, was, Ben Schindler. Since Master acquired me I am simply known now as Slave. I'm thirty-five years old now. I celebrated my birthday by having Master give my butt thirty-five hard swats with his leather paddle. Then he lashed me to an extra long massage table my meat stick pulled through a hole in the center of the table and wedged a long wax candle deep into my hole. He smeared whipped cream all over my paddled and red butt cheeks and said that was my birthday cake. With my hands shackled behind me I lay there choking on my tears and thought what a fucked up way this was to celebrate my birthday… While the candle tormented my hole Master allowed some of the guys that work for him to come in the room and drive me crazy. Two guys stood at the sides of the table and licked and slurped the whipped cream off my delectable butt cheeks while two other guys squatted under the table and sucked hard at my poor aching balls. That had me screaming and wailing in agony, let me tell you. My balls are sensitive to begin with, but, being filled to overflowing with my juice makes them a hundred percent more sensitive. Those guys sucking on them nearly made me totally insane. Master's instructions allowed them to suck my balls but not to let me cum, so of course my nine-inch meat stick was off limits to them.

The night that my neighbor Freddy came knocking at my door was like any other week night. I was mentally tired from the long stressful workday and was ready to kick back and relax with a light dinner and then stretch out on my recliner in my underwear and socks and sip a cold beer while watching TV, just ordinary end of the day guy things. None of that was to be that night though. I got home at six forty five that night, a little later than I usually get home and was ready for some very much-needed relaxation. I came into my apartment dressed in an Armani pinstriped navy blue suit, my attaché case in one hand as I opened the door and my mail tucked under my arm. I dropped my attaché case on the floor, put my mail down on the coffee table without even looking at it just yet and walked to my bedroom to get undressed, shucking off my suit jacket as I went.

"Ah, what a day, what another fucked up day," I murmured as I walked into my bedroom.

I chucked my suit jacket onto my bed and undid my tie, sliding it off my shirt before sitting down to take my shoes off. As I sat there untying the laces of my shoes I wondered if the stress of working as a security chief was really worth it. I mean okay, the money was good and all that and it afforded me the luxury apartment that I lived in and the only expenses I had were for myself, seeing as I'm not married and I don't have kids, but there were days when it could really get to me. I placed my shoes on the floor next to my bed, stood up and slid my suit pants off. As I was unbuttoning my white shirt I heard the knocking at my door. Clad now in just my white dress shirt, halfway unbuttoned, my white BVD underpants and my up to the calf black nylon ribbed dress socks I stepped to the door of my bedroom.

"Yeah, who is it?" I called out loudly enough for the person at the door to hear me.

"Uh Ben, it's uh, your next door neighbor, Freddy," I heard Freddy reply, sounding a bit unsure of himself. "Do, do you think we could maybe talk a little? I could really use your advice at the moment."

"Freddy?" I asked, walking slowly to the door, unbuttoning my shirt as I went, slightly baring my hairy chest. "Uh, I just got in from work and I'm really tired and all. Could we maybe do this another time?"

In all the time I had lived in the building Freddy and I had never said more than hello and good-bye to each other in the hallway when we would see each other. Now all of a sudden he needed my advice? What could that be about I wondered. Freddy is a short guy of five feet three inches tall. He's pretty much on the portly side, almost bald and I guessed his age to be close to mine.

"Well Ben, I was just thinking that being that it's still fresh in my mind we could maybe talk about it now, Freddy said from behind my closed and locked door. "You see she just called and said some very upsetting things to me and all. It won't take long, I promise."

I took a deep breath, undid the lock on the door and opened it slightly.

"Freddy, I just got in from work, I'm in just my damned shirt, under shorts and socks here," I said, sounding a little more than irritated, not knowing that I had saved him the trouble of having to strip me. "Is it really that important man?"

"She, she's threatening me Ben," he said through quivering lips. "I really need some advice on how to handle this. I mean, you told me once that you were a security chief and all, so I figured that maybe you could help me out. I'm figuring that you know the laws on stuff and all." "Okay Freddy, come on in," I said, opening the door all the way and he stepped in. "Let me just get into a pair of gym shorts or something. Sitting here in my underpants doesn't seem all that appropriate."

I closed the door and started walking toward my bedroom. I wondered what the fuck kind of trouble a dorky and nerdy guy like Freddy could possibly have gotten into.

"Uh Ben, would you like me to pour us a drink?" Freddy asked, noticing my extensive bar in the living room.

"Yeah sure, help yourself," I replied, still sounding a bit miffed but knowing that a drink would calm me down. "I'll have scotch, two cubes. The refrigerator is behind the bar."

"Thanks Ben, you're a real pal," Freddy said.

"Yeah, good old Ben," I whispered angrily.

I padded to my bedroom on my socked feet, fished a pair of blue gym shorts out of a drawer and pulled them on.

"Freddy, I'm just going to use the bathroom," I called out, later realizing what a mistake that was as it gave him the time to slip the pills into my scotch. "I'll be out in a minute or two."

"Take your time," Freddy called back and dropped two tiny pills into my scotch.

They dissolved instantly. Sitting there in the bathroom with my gym shorts and underpants around my ankles I pulled my socks back up to my calves and wondered just what the hell kind of trouble Freddy had gotten himself into. What I didn't know as I sat there farting and shitting was the kind of trouble I was about to fall into. I was going to be in the soup as some guys call it…

When I was done in the bathroom I padded back out to the living room. Freddy was seated on my couch his drink in hand, my drink waiting on the coffee table.

"I really appreciate this Ben," he said as I sat down next to him, picked up my drink and crossed one leg, my black socked foot resting on my knee. "I promise this won't take long."

"What kind of trouble are you in?" I asked him, trying to get right to the point and took long sip of my drink.

"Well, a few weeks ago I met this girl, a very beautiful girl," Freddy began and I took another sip of my drink. "Her name is Linda. You might want to remember that for future reference."

"Okay, Linda, duly noted," I said with a fake smile and tapped the side of my head.

"Yeah, now we had a couple of dates and I slept with her once," Freddy went on. "And from all points it looks like that's all it's going to be, once."

"Before you go on, how did you meet this girl?" I asked him, sipped my drink and my head spun.

"Well, I'm sort of ashamed to say that I met her through a personal ad," Freddy replied as I rubbed my eyes with my fingertips, starting to feel woozy, very woozy. "I know that personal ads can be dangerous Ben. And I think I found that out the hard way. As I said we had a couple of dates and I slept with her once."

"Y-yeah, you said that," I said and raised my glass to my lips.

If I didn't know better I would swear that Freddy was helping me get the glass to my lips. As he held the glass to my mouth I gulped down what was left of my scotch. Freddy took the glass from me and placed it on the coffee table in front of us. As I yawned I realized that he hadn't touched his drink.

"Ohhhhh man, sorry Freddy," I apologized as I yawned, leaning back on the couch. "It's not you man, just that I had a long and stressful day."

"I'm sure you did Ben," Freddy said and curled a hand around my socked ankle resting on my knee. "I mean, being a security chief and all can't be all that easy."

"Th-that's for sure," I stammered and grinned as he squeezed my socked foot. "Careful man, I'm a bit on the ticklish side."

I wasn't all that thrilled that the guy was in my apartment, I was even less thrilled that he was holding tightly to my damned-socked foot. But for the life of me I couldn't bring myself to ask him to let go. Fuck, I couldn't bring myself to move.

"S-so tell me what happened a-after you slept with, Lind-Linda," I stammered stupidly, doing my very best to stay awake at that point.

"Well, as I said we slept together just that once," Freddy repeated again.

"Yea-yeah, you said that," I said softly, looking at him now through blurred vision.

"And now she's claiming that I raped her," Freddy said. "Can you believe that Ben? I mean, I take the girl out to dinner, take her to a movie, she invites me back up to her place and then she accuses me of rape. I mean, what kind of girl does a thing like that Ben?"

I couldn't answer at that point because the drug that had been in my scotch had taken effect. I was in a state of total incomprehension at that point. I wasn't exactly asleep, but I was not exactly awake either.

"Ben?" Freddy asked again and squeezed my foot tighter.

Smiling triumphantly Ben let go of my foot and pushed it down onto the floor. I sat there with my head lolling back and my mouth wide open, my eyes mostly closed. Quickly, Ben stood up and got a straight-backed chair from my kitchen and brought it into the living room. Then, he reached under me, hoisted me off the couch and into his arms and stood there laughing insanely as I lay limp as a rag doll in his strong arms…

I knew the guy was carrying me over to the chair, I knew I'd been had, horribly, but there was nothing I could do to defend myself. Fuck, what was that shit he'd put in my drink? And what about Linda???

When I came to a long while later it was two AM on the dot. At least according to the digital clock on my VCR it was two AM. God, had I conked out and slept for almost seven hours in my living room? My vision cleared and I looked up to see Freddy sitting on my couch, a food stained plate on the coffee table in front of him. Not only had the guy invaded my privacy, but he'd made and eaten dinner in my apartment as well. Just what the fuck was up with this guy I wondered?

"Wh-what happened?" I murmured softly and tried to stand up, but that was of course impossible as Freddy had me securely roped to the chair I was seated in. "H-hey, wh-what the fuck is going on here Freddy? Wh-why am I all tied up like this?"

My arms were pulled behind me and roped tightly at the wrists with mounds upon mounds of knotted rope around them and also tied to one of the straight rungs on the back of the chair keeping my hands totally immobilized. Tightly tied rope was wound over and over my upper body, pinning me to the chair, my white shirt was off me and my big fat pink nipples left visible. Actually the way Freddy had tied my upper body to the chair sure made a nice showcase of my nipples I have to say. Fuck, I have nipples fatter than a woman's; so many times my buddies at the gym would make sport in the locker room, seeing who could get a good grab and really squeeze the fuck out of my big man tits, but alas, that's a story for another time. My gym shorts were off me as well and my big nine-inch meat stick and my over-sized hairy balls were sticking out of the fly opening of my BVD under shorts. My meat stick was fear hard and pointing straight up at the ceiling as I took in my dreadful situation. My legs were spread apart and my socked feet were each lashed tightly at the ankles to the legs of the chair. A good amount of rope was also tied over and over my thighs, holding them down to the chair. Fuck, I couldn't move an inch. Freddy had me better than totally immobilized.

"Stay calm and I will gladly explain everything to you Ben," Freddy said and I looked at my empty scotch glass on the coffee table.

"Y-you bastard, you drugged my drink," I said in disbelief, looking down at my hardness in all it's glory. "Fucking pervert, if you wanted my damned dick you could have approached me in another way man."

Freddy smiled and got to his feet.

"It's true that I want your dick Ben," Freddy said, stepping behind me and placing his hands on my muscular shoulders, squeezing them tight. "But the man who ordered you wants it and other parts of you even more."

"What the fuck are you talking about man?" I asked him angrily.

"You came here claiming you were in trouble with some girl named Linda."

"Well, I needed a way to get into your apartment didn't I?" Freddy asked and moved a hand to the back of my big neck, squeezing it gently. "I must say Mr. Gunther is going to be extremely happy with you Ben. I of course am going to miss you as my next door neighbor. But eventually someone will move in here I'm sure."

"Freddy, what the fuck are you talking about?" I asked him, my heart starting to pound in total fear. "I'm not moving out or anything like that. Now, untie me, get the fuck out of here and I'll try to forget this ever happened. Fuck man, I can't believe this happened. Look at the fucked up position you've got me in. Tied up in my damned under shorts and socks, god! If you wanted to have a kinky experience all you had to do was say so and I would have sent you somewhere real nice man!!"

Freddy let go of the back of my neck and stepped in front of me, looking down at me adoringly, smiling and shaking his head "no" from side to side.

"It's not as simple as that," he said. "You see Ben, you are moving out."

I gulped hard and looked up at him beseechingly.

"Will you at least tell me what the fuck this is all about?" I asked him in a practical fear-filled whisper. "Just what are you planning on doing with me Freddy?"

I figured I needed time to try to get myself untied. It was the only way to take the fucker down after all. I would have to keep him talking for as long as possible. But at two AM how long could I possibly keep him talking?

"You see Ben, I work for what is known as an import and export business," Freddy said, squatting down in front of me and sticking a finger in the top of one of my socks, rubbing his fingertip against the skin of my leg under it. "But, for a security chief such as yourself I'm sure you have other terms for the business I'm in."

"Wh-white slavery," I croaked miserably and flexed my wrists in the ropes.

The rope held fast, *fuck!*

"Yes Ben, white slavery," Ben said and snapped the elastic in my sock against my calf, moving his hand to my big balls, tugging them gently. "The organization I work for is very secret and very, very underground. When a rich customer decides on the type of person he or she would like to own we fill that need. The person in the organization who knows of someone who fits the customer's bill makes it that much easier all around for filling that customer's need. You are a case in point."

I tried to ignore the fact that the guy was tugging and fucking sniffing at my damned balls.

"Wh-why am I a case in point?" I asked desperately, fearing the answer I would get. "Who would want to buy an average guy like me?"

"Now Ben, you are a little more than average, at least I would say you are," Freddy said and brazenly slurped and kissed my balls, getting a good breathless gasp out of me.

"Ohhhhhrr god man, easy with my nuts you fucker," I rasped angrily. "I have real sensitive balls."

"More than six feet tall, handsome as a devil, built superbly, you are above average Ben," Freddy said and stood up over me. "Don't sell yourself short. And that big tube steak between your legs is reason enough to up the price that I'm getting for you Ben. When the man who purchased you sees that he's going to be very impressed I am sure."

"You mean to tell me that you've done this sort of thing before?" I asked him. "Literally kidnapped men and women and handed them over to your so-called customers?"

"I wouldn't say handed over Ben," Freddy corrected me. "We sold them to our customers."

I gulped hard again and curled my toes back under my socks.

"Wh-where are these people now?" I asked him through clenched teeth. "What became of them?"

"Well, more than likely they learned to serve their masters," Freddy said. "As you will eventually learn too Ben."

He turned away from me and walked over to the bar. I watched through horror filled eyes as he poured himself a glass of scotch.

"Wh-where have you sent these people?" I asked him softly as he sipped his scotch and set the glass down on the bar.

"Many places," Freddy said as he made his way back over to me. "We package them up in big crates and ship them wherever the customer happens to be."

"How do your customers learn of your services?" I asked, trembling in my socks by then.

"Various ways, mostly through word of mouth," Ben replied, standing next to me and curling a hand again around the back of my neck. "Our clientele is a very elite group of very well to do men and women Ben. They are not your average Joe's on the street or middle class workers."

"Freddy, this is insanity," I said, looking up at him, about to ask him the million dollar question. "Wh-where are you planning on sending me?"

"I'm not planning on it Ben, I'm going to do it," he said, taking a wad of duct tape from his pocket. "You my friend are going to be going to Iraq to serve one of our very distinguished ambassadors who has grown very bored of being alone."

"I-Iraq???" I gasped loudly and just as I raised my voice Freddy slapped the wad of duct tape tightly over my mouth, thoroughly gagging me. "RRRRmmmmffff!!!"

As he pressed the tape against my lips and mustache I was looking at him with my eyes opened wide in more than out right horror.

"Now Ben, I want you to relax," Freddy said. "The man who ordered you is going to take good care of you, very good care actually. After his term as ambassador is over I'm sure he'll bring you back to the United States with him so you can belong to him here as well. Or, he may just sell you for double of what he bought you for to one of those insane Iraqis over there."

As he spoke Freddy walked back over to the bar.

"RRRmmmmffffff!!!" I sputtered wildly; thrashing wildly in the chair, desperate now to get myself untied and pummel the fucking guy.

Iraq? The fucker was planning on sending me to a Middle Eastern country for the rest of my life? No way! No fucking way!

"Now Ben, I want you to relax and stop that struggling," Ben admonished me and sipped his drink. "The way I have you tied there's no way you're going anywhere, except where I send you of course."

Ignoring him, I pressed my muscular chest forward, straining mightily against the ropes holding me to the chair.

“RRRRRRfffffff!!!!” I roared behind my gag.

“Hmmm, seems like I’ll have to calm you down myself I see,” Freddy said with distaste and my eyes opened even wider in horror as he produced a syringe and a length of elastic.

I shook my head madly “no” from side to side as Freddy stepped back over to me and tied the elastic tightly around the center of my left arm, the syringe in his back pocket. He tapped lightly on my arm till a thick vein showed itself.

“Very nice, very nice indeed, good muscular arms,” Freddy said. “I really should make the customer pay more than what I’m getting for you Ben.”

He took the syringe from his pocket and pressed the tip of the needle into my popped up vein. I winced at the pinch and then watched as the fucker depressed the plunger.

“This is simply going to relax you Ben,” Freddy said reassuringly as he fed whatever it was slowly into my vein. “I’m not putting you to sleep or anything, at least not yet.”

As the stuff trickled into me I stopped struggling and felt a warming like sensation course through me. A few seconds after that I felt as if I was sort of floating in the chair I was tied to. Freddy took the needle out of my arm and removed the elastic. A tiny red dot remained where he’d injected me.

“There, feeling better?” he asked me, placing the syringe and the elastic on the coffee table.

Smiling, he stood over me.

“You really are an extremely handsome man Ben,” he said, hooking a finger under the duct tape gag. “I really wish I could afford to buy you for myself.”

Smiling, he began peeling the gag off me, the sticky duct tape pulling meanly and painfully on my thick mustache.

"Arrrrrrhhhh," I ranted softly as the gag came off me.

"There, now that I've calmed you I doubt you'll be able to make much noise Ben," Freddy said, tossing the gag onto the coffee table as well.

I saw that clumps of my mustache had been pulled out and stuck to the gag. God!

"F-Freddy, stop this now," I said softly. "Let me go man. You'll go to jail for this, mark my words."

"I doubt that very much Ben," Freddy said. "You see, even a very wealthy policeman in high ranks purchased someone from our organization some time back. Linda has belonged to that high-ranking officer for more than a couple of years now. So I truly doubt that even the police could get you out of the soup, so to speak."

Realizing that with more and more mounting horror just how helpless my situation was I lolled my head back and choked back tears. He was right, the way he had phrased it a moment ago, I was in the soup and sinking fast.

"Wh-when am I to be shipped out Freddy?" I asked him, looking up at the ceiling.

"By six AM this morning," he replied, glancing over at the clock on my VCR. "In less than four hours from now you'll be packed up in a crate good and tight and on a plane bound for the Middle East."

This could not be happening I told myself. This was a nightmare, fuck, this was worse than a nightmare. Is this what I had gone to college for? Is this what I had worked and labored so hard for? To be kidnapped and sold to some unknown wealthy ambassador and kept as his sexual play toy?

"Fr-Freddy, listen, listen to me man," I said through trembling lips, leaning my head back down and facing forward. "Y-you can't sell me to some guy. I mean, I'm not even gay man."

"Who said anything about sexual preferences Ben?" Freddy asked. "This has nothing to do with that. This has to do with satisfying a customer's need."

"And this customer specifically requested *me?"* I asked through clenched teeth as whatever he injected me with had my body swooning.

"Well no, he didn't exactly request Ben Schindler per se," Freddy said, squatting in front of me, gripped my thighs and stole a few long licks on my big hairy balls as they rested on the seat of the chair I was bound to.

"Uhhhhhrrr, g-god man, ea-easy with my nuts," I said breathlessly.

"The man you will belong to put in an order for a man of about your age," Freddy said, flicking his tongue over my balls in between speaking, sniffing them at the same time. "He wants a man of six feet tall or more, he wants him to have dark hair and a thick mustache and he's to work in some sort of police capacity. You as a security chief fit the bill perfectly."

"God almighty," I whispered.

"When I told my superiors that my next door neighbor filled the order request to a tee it was decided," Freddy said, not looking up at me.

Then, to my horror and mortification he slid his hands down to my calves, gripped them just above my socks and slowly, so slowly slid his open mouth down over my fear hard dick.

"Ohhhhh no, no, not this Freddy, d-don't be sucking my meat stick man," I whimpered miserably, yet loved the feel of what he was doing to me all at the same time. (For the moment it took my mind off my impending horrible fate.) "Ohhhhhrrr God, you fucker!"

Ignoring me Freddy pursed his lips tightly around the sexy crown of my meat stick, held it like that and poked his tongue tip teasingly against my wide slit. Pre cum oozed from me and Freddy slicked it onto his tongue and gulped it down, keeping his pursed lips wrapped tightly around the crown of my meat stick, driving me batty.

"Ohhhhhrrr god, y-you pervert," I whispered and shuddered involuntarily in the chair.

He swirled and swiveled his tongue over and over the crown of my meat stick, eating my pre cum as it oozed and oozed from me.

"Ohhhhhh fuccccckkkk, Fr-Freddy, wh-why are you doing this to me?" I whimpered.

"I always like to sample the merchandise that I sell," he said, momentarily looking up at me, his hands holding tightly to my calves just above my socks.

"Th-that isn't what I meant man," I seethed and curled my tied hands into fists as he slid his mouth down the throbbing shaft of my meat stick. "Ohhhhhrrrr god man, th-there's no denying that that feels great."

I grimaced in a mixture of ecstasy and helplessness and curled my toes back under my socks as Freddy's mouth made magic happen to my meat stick. Unbelievably the guy was able to get the entire length of my pride and joy down into his throat not an easy task let me tell you.

"G-god Freddy, I'm getting close already man!!" I garbled.

My body felt like it was floating on the chair. I guessed that was because of the drugs he had given me. I was in a state of dizziness and ecstasy all at the same time as the guy sucked the fuck out of my meat stick. His head bobbed up and down, his lips crashing against my thick nest of curly pubic hair and my big guy pounded like crazy in his mouth as he suckled me and suckled me.

"Ohhhhrrr fucccckkk, this, this is insanity man, but, but, I'm going to shoot my load like gangbusters you pervert!" I panted like crazy and a geyser of my man juices erupted from me. "Ohhhhhh yeah, fucking A!"

I leaned my head back and looked up at the ceiling as Freddy gulped down my torrents of creamy sperm, gasping for breath as the guy sucked me and sucked me. He didn't lose a drop of my juices. The fucker swallowed every drop of me.

"Ohhhhhrrrr," I garbled in the forced ecstasy.

When I was done Freddy let my dick slip slowly from his mouth, smacking his lips around it, the remnants of my cum on his lips. I looked back down and watched as he lifted my balls into his hand and gave them a light squeeze and a tug.

"Ea-easy with my balls man," I said softly. "They're always all sensitive after I've just shot a load."

"I'm truly glad you enjoyed that Ben," Freddy said, gently squeezing and tugging on my balls, keeping my manhood semi hard between my legs. "The man you're going to belong to isn't going to allow you to shoot your load all that often. I hear he insists on almost constant restraint in that area. Of course he'll use you to get him off almost on a daily basis I am sure. But as for your needs in that arena I hear that he plans to keep you hard and frustrated at all times."

A feeling of dread swooned over me as more and more I was realizing this was no damned joke. I was really in the soup here. I looked longingly over at my attaché case where I had dropped it earlier as I came in the door from work, knowing that my gun was in there, totally out of my reach. Then, Freddy let go of my balls, leaned down and slurped my semi hardness into his mouth a second time.

"Ohhhhhhh fuck, oh god Freddy," I gasped throatily. "N-not again so soon. Shit man, I'm all sensitive and sexy after I've just shot a load man!"

Freddy's tongue worked magic in getting my nine-inch guy standing up at attention again. He sucked me like crazy till he got a second load of my juices out of me.

"Ohhhhhrrrr fuck, you pervert, got me creaming like a bitch in heat all over again man," I snarled and this time after Freddy let my meat stick slip out of his mouth he produced a tight fitting cock ring. He snapped it on me, just under the base of my balls and around my dick, keeping me good and painfully hard.

"Huuuuuhhh, ohhhhrrr shit, Fr-Freddy, what's the point of all *this*?" I asked miserably, looking down at my poor dick as it throbbed long and hard between my legs, beads of piss now oozing from my slit.

"Just want you to start getting used to your new and frustrating status Ben," Freddy said, getting to his feet and picking up the wad of duct tape. "The man that you're going to belong to expects you to arrive sexually frustrated and very, very horny. Keeping a man hard after he's cum twice is a sure-fire way of insuring just that. Now no more talking Ben, it's time for me to start preparing you for shipment."

"Fr-Freddy pl-please reconsider what you're doin.... mmmmffff..." I said and then he pressed the duct tape over my mouth, silencing me. "Mmmmmmmfffff!!!!"

Stepping behind me Freddy reached around me and grabbed my nipples his in his thumbs and first two fingers.

"Oh Ben, I sure am going to miss you as a neighbor," Freddy whispered. "But the money I'm getting for you will surely compensate for my loss."

He squeezed and twisted my nipples and gave one of my earlobes a lick before letting go of them. Besides having very sensitive balls I also have extremely sensitive nipples. A girl I dated a long time ago discovered that if she squeezed and twisted my big fat nipples I would get hard in seconds. She called my nipples the control knobs for my cock. I called them my man tits…

"Your master is also going to love these big over-sized tits of yours I might add," Freddy said and stepped back over to the (my?) bar. "I'm sure he'll make you wear tit clamps more often than not. Actually, knowing his sadistic nature I'm more than sure of it."

My meat stick raged big and hard between my legs, pointing straight up at the ceiling. Never before had I shot two loads in such short succession. Never before had I been so hard and frustrated feeling after having shot my load. Never before had I been in such a fucked up predicament. Never before had I thought of my big man tits being clamped more often than not. Even that girl I met a while back, Rebecca was her name if I remember correctly. Even Rebecca who loved to tie me up took the tit clamps off me after a few hours. God! But like my buddies playing at grabbing my tits in the locker room that's a story for another time. I watched as Freddy poured himself another glass of scotch, helping himself to my best stuff. Smiling over at me he sipped his drink and then placed the glass atop the bar. I looked around my apartment and realized, really and truly realized that if Freddy carried out this diabolical plan I would never see this place again. I thought about my friends, my CO-workers and most of all my family. Would everyone think I had just disappeared of my own accord or would someone be smart enough to contact the authorities? Fuck, even if someone did contact the authorities who would think to search for me in Iraq of all places? Then, from his pocket Freddy produced another syringe. I watched as he filled it from a small bottle of amber colored liquid.

"Mmmmffffff…" I whimpered.

"Not to worry Ben, this is not harmful in any way, it's simply a very potent aphrodisiac," Ben said, grinning over at me from the bar. "It's a mixture of herbs from the orient, multi vitamins and an equivalent of the stuff that people use to stay awake at night, all adding up to a very powerful Spanish fly."

He finished filling the syringe and came back over to me with it. He placed it on the chair between my legs and again tied the elastic tightly around my arm.

"Mmmmfffff…" I sputtered as he tapped at my arm with his fingertips, getting a vein up and very visible.

He injected the aphrodisiac into my vein, slowly pushing the plunger down on the syringe.

"Yes Ben, you are going to arrive very horny and very ready to serve your master's needs," Freddy said. "You should feel this taking effect within a few minutes."

It took even less time than that. When the syringe was empty I suddenly felt my heart racing, I broke out in goose bumps and my meat stick throbbed a thousand times faster than it had been doing already.

"Rrrrmmmffffff!!" I gasped fitfully behind the duct tape gag. "Hhhhrrrrmmmmffff…"

"Feeling it already eh Ben?" Freddy asked me teasingly and closed a hand around my big manhood as it oozed and oozed pre cum. "Oh yes, if I were to jack you off now Ben you would shoot torrents of cream that you didn't know you were capable of."

When he let go of my dick the feeling intensified still more.

“mmmmmffffff…” I whimpered as I sat there feeling totally helpless and totally horny.

My nipples came to strange life on my chest and tingled like crazy. I again curled my toes back under my socks and began sweating in the strange and crazy ecstasy. Freddy took still another small bottle of liquid from his pocket and again filled the syringe.

“RRRRRMMMMfffff…” I ranted at him.

“It’s another sedative Ben,” he explained calmly. “I need to get you very tired now, very, very tired. It’s time to get you packed up and ready to go. I want everything ready for when the van arrives in a few hours. Not to mention that I need to get some sleep.”

He again injected me in the popped vein and this time gave me what felt like more than double the dose of the sedative from earlier. My head began spinning even before he was done injecting me.

“mmmmmm…” I crooned as I felt myself drifting away, feeling like I was floating on a cloud.

When he was done injecting the stuff into me Freddy took the elastic off my arm and got to his feet, looking down at me. My head lolled back and my eyes closed halfway.

“Very good,” Freddy said and stroked my hair. “Very good indeed. Now, don’t go away Ben, I will be back in a jiffy.”

Laughing meanly Freddy put the syringe down on the bar and beat a hasty retreat from my apartment. Where the fuck was he going I wondered miserably as I drifted still further into a dizzying stupor. As I sat there more asleep, much more asleep than awake I thought about trying to get myself untied. I thought about trying to get myself over to my attaché case and get my gun from it. I thought about arresting Freddy and organizing a search party for all the abducted men and women he’d told me about. But thoughts were all these things were.

Sitting there tied, drugged and totally helpless there was nothing I could do for myself, let alone for all the abducted men and women. My eyes closed and I fell fully asleep…

It was five thirty AM when I came to, still more in a stupor than awake. I realized that I had slept tied to the chair and no doubt Freddy had slept the few hours in his apartment. But horror of horrors awoke me some more as I saw the coffin like wooden crate a few feet from where I was seated. Fuck, he must have dragged it in during the night while I was sleeping off the drugs he had given me. My meat stick pounded big and hard between my legs, big and piss hard to be exact. With tears welled up in my eyes I looked with utter dismay at the crate, knowing that I would soon be in it. That is unless I was able to do something to get myself out of this fucked up mess.

"Mmmmffff…" I whimpered and suddenly heard the voices coming from my kitchen.

"I think we'd better get him packed up now and ready," I heard Freddy saying. "Chances are the van that Mister Gunther is sending will be here early."

"Damn it man Freddy, I want just one sample of that big tube steak of his," I heard a deep male voice saying in earnest. "I mean I'm straight as a fucking arrow and all that, but fuck, watching a guy with a big schlong like the one that guy out there has shoot his load is really something to see. And the way you got him all roped up in just his underpants and socks is real sexy for some fucking reason."

"I told you no," Freddy said, sounding exasperated as he and two big guys, built like linebackers exited my kitchen and made their way into my living room. "We have to send him to Mr. Gunther very horny and very frustrated. With the dose of the aphrodisiac I gave him a few hours ago that has been very well accomplished. And I don't want anything to ruin it."

The three men stopped in their tracks when they saw I was awake, somewhat and leering angrily and insanely at them. Sweat dripped off my forehead, ran down my temples and seeped into the tiny spaces between my duct tape gag and skin.

"Ah, he's awake," Freddy said. "Ben, meet your packers."

"RRRRRMMMMFFFF!!!!" I snarled angrily at them as big beads of piss slid down my throbbing shaft.

"I'm glad you guys are here for the packaging part," Freddy said, taking a syringe from his pocket. "Should I drug him just to be on the safe side?"

"Nah," one of the linebackers said with a grin. "I like it better when they put up a struggle. And besides, you want him alert and ready to serve your customer when he arrives. I'm sure he'll sleep a lot during the flight."

I shivered in a fear I never knew before as the two men approached the chair and Freddy pried the heavy wooden lid off the crate. I gulped hard behind my gag when I saw the contents of the padded crate. There were small air holes on the sides of the thing that I hadn't noticed before and it was marked "Contents: Sedated Wild Animal Enclosed. Handle with Care" on the sides as well.

"Now Mr. Schindley, or whatever the fuck your name is," the first linebacker said to me and grabbed a handful of my hair, yanking my head back.

"RRRRmmmmffff!!!" I snarled up at him as he looked maniacally down into my tear filled eyes.

"We can do this the easy way, which is you simply cooperate and let us do our work in getting you packed and ready," he said to me, pulling hard on my hair. "Or we can do it the hard way, with you struggling and fighting us. But I assure you, either way we do it, you are going to be packaged and put in that crate for shipment."

He leaned down and kissed my gagged mouth. I felt as if I had just been given the kiss of death. My legs felt like they had turned to jelly as fear coursed through my very being, a fear that was born of a sick insanity. As the two linebackers type men began untying me from the chair, starting down at my feet Freddy took the packaging materials out of the crate, starting with some articles of what looked like tight fitting leather clothing and thick leather straps of varying lengths and widths.

"Heh, he sure is a sexy guy huh?" the first linebacker asked his buddy as they untied my socked feet from the chair. "Mr. Gunther sure is going to love him."

The two men laughed meanly and then untied my thighs. I stretched my long legs out at my sides and I have to say it felt great to be able to move them again. But I knew that if I didn't make a move soon I would be tied up all over again and this time immobilized even worse. They got to their feet and untied the rope wound over and over my upper muscular body. The first linebacker, the guy who made such a fuss over the fact of how straight he was gave one of my nipples a mean squeeze and a twist.

"RRRmmmmmffff!!!" I rasped at him.

"Nice tits you got there Boy," he snickered in my face and again kissed my gagged mouth.

"Perhaps we should leave his hands roped behind him while we get him packaged," Freddy said, sounding slightly nervous as he held a big fat pink butt plug in hand.

I didn't need three guesses to know where that thing was going.

"Relax Freddy, not to worry," the second linebacker said reassuringly as the rope around my wrists was being undone. "We have this situation totally under control."

When the rope fell away from my wrists the two men quickly grabbed my upper and lower arms and hoisted me meanly out of the chair.

"HHHHrrrrrmmmffff!!!" I sputtered maniacally and struggled like a madman in their strong grasps. "Fr-fruckers…"

I looked at Freddy with a crazed glean in my eyes as he nervously approached with that big butt plug in hand.

"Okay Freddy boy, lets get this show on the road," the first linebacker said as he held tightly to my muscular left arm. "Time is wasting and Mr. Gunther is waiting. Get that thing wedged up in him good and tight."

Freddy stepped behind me and tore my BVD under shorts off me, leaving me clad for the moment in just my socks, a cock ring and a gag.

"Spread those sexy legs good and wide Mr. Schindley, or whatever the fuck your name isn't anymore," the first linebacker ordered me. "We have to cut off your bathroom needs for a day or so."

He gave my ankle a hard kick with the toe of his steel-booted foot and I involuntarily did as I had just been told.

"Hrrrrrmmmmfffff!!!" I seethed as Freddy wedged the butt plug slowly and deeply into my hole.

My head spun as the slightly lubricated thing invaded me. I had the strange feeling that he had lubricated the sides of the thing with oil that he had found in my kitchen. It rubbed slimy and painfully against the walls of my hole as it was pushed into me. I arched my muscular body forward and grimaced miserably behind my gag as Freddy gave the thing a few mean turns as he got it good and tight inside me. I felt more stopped up than a clogged drain.

"Man oh man, I just love when they struggle like this," the second linebacker said snidely. "Makes it all worthwhile, not to mention how horny it gets me."

"I couldn't agree more," his buddy said and just for the fuck of it the two men hoisted me a few inches off the floor.

Freddy stepped in front of me and held up a thin clear tube. The thing resembled a catheter. It was something my master would keep in my pee hole pretty often. Only the one Freddy had in hand was sealed off on one end.

"Okay you guys hold him tight now, real tight," Freddy said cautiously. "This thing going inside him is going to have him screaming in bloody agony."

"Rmmmmffffff…" I garbled, shaking my head "no" wildly from side to side as my socked feet dangled off the floor and Freddy grabbed a handful of my balls.

Slowly, so slowly, he slid the thin tube into my poor dick hole.

"HHHHHrrrrrrmmmmmffffff!!!!!" I screeched and leaned my head back, sweating in my socks as the two men held me effortlessly aloft.

The thing going into my piss hole felt totally invasive and drove me batty like I can't describe to you. It totally cut off my need to piss and the pressure in my meat stick was immense.

"Okay you guys, now I'll start getting him dressed for the trip," Freddy said and picked up a pair of what looked like tight fitting leather pants that had been in the crate.

Actually they were a pair of tight fitting leather pants, only that the pants were stitched together good and firmly, thus preventing the wearer of them from walking and keeping him hobbled. At the bottom of them there was a single stir-up. Freddy squatted in front of me and I didn't struggle as he began pulling the pants on over my legs. Looking down I watched as Freddy dressed me. When the leather pants were up to my thighs Freddy dashed behind me and pulled them up the rest of the way, rubbing his crotch against my rear end. My hard meat stick and balls he left sticking out of the fly opening. What a sight that made let me tell you. My poor dick with that tube wedged inside it was good and fucking hard and juicy and my sweaty balls sticking out of those tight fitting leather pants, GOD! Any girl or faggot would have gone crazy for sure. When the pants were good and snugly on me Freddy squatted down again and slipped the stir-up under the bottoms of my black socked feet. He then picked up a few of the leather straps. Quickly and efficiently he secured straps around my ankles, my thighs, my knees and an extra thick heavy-duty one around my thighs. My legs encased in those leather pants were now completely immobilized.

"Okay guys you can put him down on his feet now," Freddy said, standing up and taking a leather tee shirt out of the crate. "But keep him balanced. The way his legs are all wrapped up there's no way he can stand up on his own."

Smiling, the two men leaned in close to me and hefted my arms up so that Freddy could get the very tight fitting leather shirt onto me. He forced it over my muscular torso and the fucking thing hugged me erotically. The leather pressed against my big nipples sent chills upon chills through me, making my visible dick twitch and ooze more and more pre cum. When I saw the leather straitjacket that Freddy took from the crate my heart really sank. Moments later I was totally clad in the black leather clothing that Freddy had dressed me in. The straitjacket kept my arms yanked over my upper body and was tied tightly in the back. Freddy and his two packers added straps over the straitjacket to insure my total immobilization. Tears of fear flowed freely from my eyes and down my cheeks.

"Looking good Mr. Schindley, or whatever the fuck your name isn't anymore," the first linebacker teased me again and gave my ass a hard slap.

"RRRRmmmffff!!!" I sputtered at him.

"Okay, now for the finishing touches," Freddy said and held up a ball gag and a leather hood with eye coverings.

When I saw those things all hope died. I knew this situation was hopeless. *I was going to belong to some rich man named Mr. Gunther in a Middle Eastern country.*

"Take that duct tape off his mouth," Freddy said and the second linebacker meanly tore the tape off me.

"Arrrhhhhh!!!" I rasped throatily as again clumps of my mustache were yanked meanly out. *"Fr-Freddy, you monster, you twisted bastard!!"*

Stepping behind me Freddy put the ball gag on me. It filled my mouth, keeping my jaws open, making me unable to utter a sound. It had a tiny hole in the center of it for breathing purposes.

"I would concentrate on getting comfortable with breathing through that thin hole in your ball gag Ben," Freddy said to me mockingly. "Rather than calling me names."

He tied the ball gag securely on me behind my big neck, thoroughly silencing me, and then held up the leather hood with the eye coverings.

"Take a good last look around Ben," Freddy said to me before pulling the hood over my eyes. "I assure you this is going to be the last time you see your apartment."

I creased my eyes shut and opened them again as tears of rage and agony flowed from them. I whimpered and sobbed miserably at what my life had and would come down to. Then, Freddy slid the hood over my head, snapped the eye coverings closed and zipped it up tight in the back.

"There, he's all set to go," Freddy said, sounding satisfied.

"We're just going to leave his dick sticking out like that?" I heard the first linebacker ask.

"Yes we are," Freddy said and I felt someone tug on my balls. "When Mr. Gunther opens the crate I want that to be the first thing he sees. He'll realize that his new possession is worth every penny that he paid for it. Now, get him into the crate and then get the crate to the airport."

Strong arms lifted me by my upper body and legs and then I felt myself being lowered into the padded crate in a prone position on my back. I shuddered involuntarily and in absolute fear when I heard the heavy lid of the crate put on and pounded shut…

I must have blacked out from fear because the next thing I realized I heard a plane taking off and I got that feeling in my stomach that I always get upon take-off…

I guessed that I was in the cargo hull of the plane that was taking me to my new home…

So, as I said at the outset of this letter I have lived with Master now for a little more than a year. He keeps me well fed and in good physical condition and… oh no, the vibrator in my hole is buzzing like crazy, which means Master wants me on the double. I will have to finish this letter at some other time and hopefully even get it in the mail… My freedom depends on it…

About the Author

Christopher Trevor was born in July 1963 and grew up in New York City. As soon as he was old enough to know how he began writing fiction and has been writing gay erotic/fetish stories for the past ten to twelve years at this point. He became an avid reader as well from the time he knew how and reads everything from fiction, to non-fiction to biographies of interesting and unusual people, people who have made a difference or who have paved the way for others. Christopher attributes his writing artistic inspiration to artists such as Etienne, Tom of Finland, Tagame, The Hun, and most notably Joe T, who Christopher has had the pleasure of speaking with and even meeting over the last few years. Christopher states, "Joe

T encouraged me to write about my fetish because I was embarrassed about it at the time. Joe T said that when we are embarrassed about something that makes it even more enticing somehow." Christopher totally agreed and never stopped writing in this genre. Erotic writers who inspired Christopher Trevor were: Tom Shaw (author of "That Day at the Quarry), C.S. White (author of Big Sur), Larry Townsend (author of countless erotic novels), and Mason Powell (author of the classic story "The Brig.")

Christopher discovered that not only did he enjoy writing erotic tales but that after his first bondage experience he had a genuine flair for it. Writing to erotic oriented magazines about his first bondage experience truly opened the floodgates for Christopher where this style of writing is concerned. Christopher thanks the handsome and muscular "Greg" for that experience way back in time. Christopher took "Creative Writing" courses every semester during his high school years and while other friends of his stopped writing what they loved to write about as time went on Christopher never let a day go by when he didn't write something... "I feel that if I don't write every day I will die," Christopher has said many times over.

Foot fetish stories and all things related; spanking fetish, erotic shaving, muscle bondage, tickle torture, and hardcore stories are just a few of the areas of gay eroticism that Christopher enjoys writing about and inspiring in others as well. As one internet buddy said to Christopher where the black socks fetish is concerned, "Until I started talking with you I never gave a thought to my socks when I got dressed for work in the morning. Now when I pull my dress socks on every morning I get a chill up my spine."

Christopher is proud of the erotic effect he has on people...

Christopher Trevor is also the author of:

The Executive Guide to Foot Fetishism and Office Discipline

1-887895-36-1

Executive Ties That Bind

1-887895-37-X

Don't! Stop! That Tickles!

1-887895-31-0

The Taming of Dominick

1-887895-45-0

Timmy and The Hong Kong Tailor

1-887895-30-2

Love, Torture and Redemption

1-887895-32-9

Timmys Ticklish Trials

978-1-887895-74-3

The Gym Instructor

978-1-887895-44-6

Milked

978-1-887895-66-8

Erotic Street Blues

978-1-887895-97-2

The Abusive Wager

978-1-887895-04-0

Terry's Appointment and Other Tickling Stories

978-1-934625-08-8

The Military File

978-1-934625-21-7

Quirks

978-1-934625-24-8

Timmy and the Evil Dr. Vonvellicator

978-1-934625-42-2

Blackmail

978-1-934625-47-7

Tickled Kink

978-1-934625-49-1

Humiliation

978-1-934625-58-3

Discipline

978-1-934625-07-1

Revenge

978-1-934625-60-6

Look for them where you bought this book, Amazon.com or TheNazcaPlainsCorp.com

www.ingramcontent.com/pod-product-compliance
Lightning Source LLC
Chambersburg PA
CBHW070757280626
47162CB00016B/1414
* 9 7 8 1 9 3 4 6 2 5 6 5 1 *